Tales of India

Tales of India

FOLKTALES FROM
Bengal, Punjab, and Tamil Nadu

ILLUSTRATIONS BY
Svabhu Kohli & Viplov Singh

CHRONICLE BOOKS
SAN FRANCISCO

Library of Congress Cataloging-in-Publication Data available.

ISBN: 978-1-4521-6591-2

Manufactured in China.

Designed by Emily Dubin and Lizzie Vaughan
Typeset in Adobe Caslon and Ndogk

10 9 8 7 6 5 4 3 2 1

Chronicle Books LLC
680 Second Street
San Francisco, California 94107
www.chroniclebooks.com

Chronicle books and gifts are available at special quantity discounts to corporations, professional associations, literacy programs, and other organizations. For details and discount information, please contact our premiums department at corporatesales@chroniclebooks.com or at 1-800-759-0190.

"'Delightful creature and most charming princess,' said she,
'you have regaled me with an excellent story.
But the night is long and tedious. Pray tell me another.'"

—REV. CHARLES SWYNNERTON, F.S.A.,
"Gholâm Badshah and His Son Ghool"

Contents

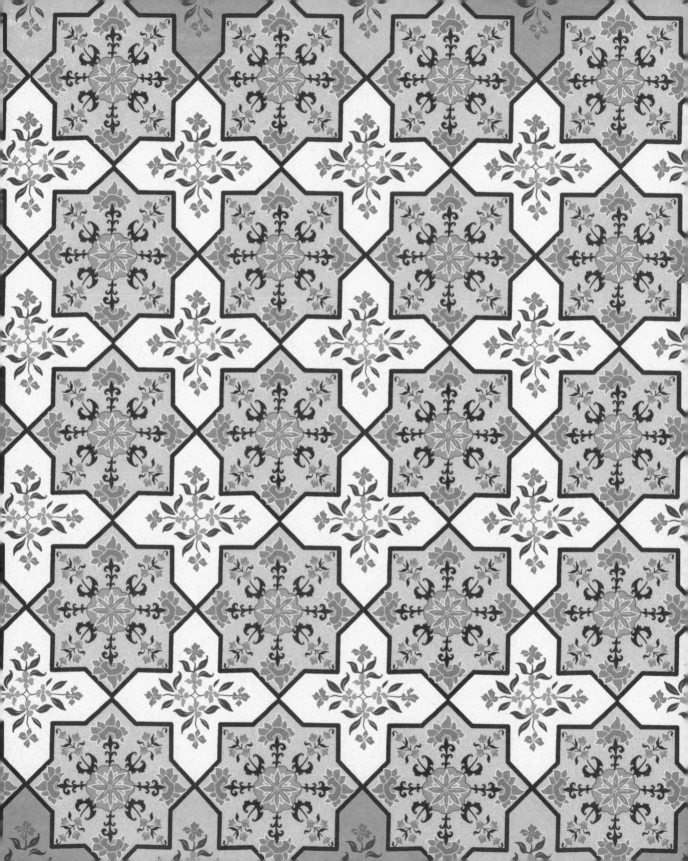

Animal Tales

THE BEAR'S
BAD BARGAIN

❧ ⋯✣⋯ ☙

Punjab

O nce upon a time, a very old woodman lived with his very old wife in a tiny hut close to the orchard of a rich man,—so close that the boughs of a pear-tree hung right over the cottage yard. Now it was agreed between the rich man and the woodman, that if any of the fruit fell into the yard, the old couple were to be allowed to eat it; so you may imagine with what hungry eyes they watched the pears ripening, and prayed for a storm of wind, or a flock of flying foxes, or anything which would cause the fruit to fall. But nothing came, and the old wife, who was a grumbling, scolding old thing, declared they would infallibly become beggars. So she took to giving her husband nothing but dry bread to eat, and insisted on his working harder than ever, till the poor old soul got quite thin; and all because the pears would not fall down! At last, the woodman turned round and declared he would not work any more unless his wife gave him *khichrî* to his dinner; so with a very bad grace the old woman took some rice and pulse, some butter and spices, and began to cook a savoury *khichrî*. What an appetising smell it had, to be sure! The woodman was for gobbling it up as soon as ever it was ready. "No, no," cried the greedy old wife, "not till you have brought me in another load of wood; and mind it is a good one. You must work for your dinner."

So the old man set off to the forest and began to hack and to hew with such a will that he soon had quite a large bundle, and with every faggot he cut he seemed to smell the savoury *khichri* and think of the feast that was coming.

Just then a bear came swinging by, with its great black nose tilted in the air, and its little keen eyes peering about; for bears, though good enough fellows on the whole, are just dreadfully inquisitive.

"Peace be with you, friend!" said the bear, "and what may you be going to do with that remarkably large bundle of wood?"

"It is for my wife," returned the woodman. "The fact is," he added confidentially, smacking his lips, "she has made *such* a *khichri* for dinner! and if I bring in a good bundle of wood she is pretty sure to give me a plentiful portion. Oh, my dear fellow, you should just smell that *khichri*!"

At this the bear's mouth began to water, for, like all bears, he was a dreadful glutton.

"Do you think your wife would give me some too, if I brought her a bundle of wood?" he asked anxiously.

"Perhaps; if it was a very big load," answered the woodman craftily.

"Would—would four hundredweight be enough?" asked the bear.

"I'm afraid not," returned the woodman, shaking his head; "you see *khichri* is an expensive dish to make,—there is rice in it, and plenty of butter, and pulse, and—"

"Would—would eight hundredweight do?"

"Say half a ton, and it's a bargain!" quoth the woodman.

"Half a ton is a large quantity!" sighed the bear.

"There is saffron in the *khichri*," remarked the woodman casually.

The bear licked his lips, and his little eyes twinkled with greed and delight.

"Well, it's a bargain! Go home sharp and tell your wife to keep the *khichri* hot; I'll be with you in a trice."

Away went the woodman in great glee to tell his wife how the bear had agreed to bring half a ton of wood in return for a share of the *khichri*.

Now the wife could not help allowing that her husband had made a good bargain, but being by nature a grumbler, she was determined not to be pleased, so she began to scold the old man for not having settled exactly the share the bear was to have; "For," said she, "he will gobble up the potful before we have finished our first helping."

On this the woodman became quite pale. "In that case," he said, "we had better begin now, and have a fair start." So without more ado they squatted down on the floor, with the brass pot full of *khichri* between them, and began to eat as fast as they could.

"Remember to leave some for the bear, wife," said the woodman, speaking with his mouth crammed full.

"Certainly, certainly," she replied, helping herself to another handful.

"My dear," cried the old woman in her turn, with her mouth so full that she could hardly speak, "remember the poor bear!"

"Certainly, certainly, my love!" returned the old man, taking another mouthful.

So it went on, till there was not a single grain left in the pot.

"What's to be done now?" said the woodman; "it is all your fault, wife, for eating so much."

"My fault!" retorted his wife scornfully, "why, you ate twice as much as I did!"

"No, I didn't!"

"Yes, you did!—men always eat more than women."

"No, they don't!"

"Yes, they do!"

"Well, it's no use quarrelling about it now," said the woodman, "the *khichri*'s gone, and the bear will be furious."

"That wouldn't matter much if we could get the wood," said the greedy old woman. "I'll tell you what we must do,—we must lock up everything there is to eat in the house, leave the *khichri* pot by the fire, and hide in the garret. When the bear comes he will think we have gone out and left his dinner for him.

Then he will throw down his bundle and come in. Of course he will rampage a little when he finds the pot is empty, but he can't do much mischief, and I don't think he will take the trouble of carrying the wood away."

So they made haste to lock up all the food and hide themselves in the garret.

Meanwhile the bear had been toiling and moiling away at his bundle of wood, which took him much longer to collect than he expected; however, at last he arrived quite exhausted at the woodcutter's cottage. Seeing the brass *khichri* pot by the fire, he threw down his load and went in. And then—mercy! wasn't he angry when he found nothing in it—not even a grain of rice, nor a tiny wee bit of pulse, but only a smell that was so uncommonly nice that he actually cried with rage and disappointment. He flew into the most dreadful temper, but though he turned the house topsy-turvy, he could not find a morsel of food. Finally, he declared he would take the wood away again, but, as the crafty old woman had imagined, when he came to the task, he did not care, even for the sake of revenge, to carry so heavy a burden.

"I won't go away empty-handed," said he to himself, seizing the *khichri* pot; "if I can't get the taste I'll have the smell!"

Now, as he left the cottage, he caught sight of the beautiful golden pears hanging over into the yard. His mouth began to water at once, for he was desperately hungry, and the pears were the first of the season; in a trice he was on the wall, up the tree, and, gathering the biggest and ripest one he could find, was just putting it into his mouth, when a thought struck him.

"If I take these pears home I shall be able to sell them for ever so much to the other bears, and then with the money I shall be able to buy some *khichri*. Ha, ha! I shall have the best of the bargain after all!"

So saying, he began to gather the ripe pears as fast as he could and put them into the *khichri* pot, but whenever he came to an unripe one he would shake his head and say, "No one would buy that, yet it is a pity to waste it." So he would pop it into his mouth and eat it, making wry faces if it was very sour.

Now all this time the woodman's wife had been watching the bear through a crevice, and holding her breath for fear of discovery; but, at last, what with being asthmatic, and having a cold in her head, she could hold it no longer, and just as the *khichrî* pot was quite full of golden ripe pears, out she came with the most tremendous sneeze you ever heard—"*A-h-che-u!*"

The bear, thinking some one had fired a gun at him, dropped the *khichrî* pot into the cottage yard, and fled into the forest as fast as his legs would carry him.

So the woodman and his wife got the *khichrî*, the wood, and the coveted pears, but the poor bear got nothing but a very bad stomach-ache from eating unripe fruit.

THE BRÂHMAN GIRL
THAT MARRIED a TIGER

❖ ┄❀┄ ❖

Tamil Nadu

In a certain village there lived an old Brâhman who had three sons
and a daughter. The girl being the youngest was brought up most
tenderly and became spoilt, and so whenever she saw a beautiful boy
she would say to her parents that she must be wedded to him. Her parents
were, therefore, much put about to devise excuses for taking her away from her
youthful lovers. Thus passed on some years, till the girl was very near attaining
her puberty and then the parents, fearing that they would be driven out of their
caste if they failed to dispose of her hand in marriage before she came to the
years of maturity, began to be eager about finding a bridegroom for her.

Now near their village there lived a fierce tiger, that had attained to great
proficiency in the art of magic, and had the power of assuming different
forms. Having a great taste for Brâhman's food, the tiger used now and then
to frequent temples and other places of public feeding in the shape of an old
famished Brâhman in order to share the food prepared for the Brâhmans. The
tiger also wanted, if possible, a Brâhman wife to take to the woods, and there
to make her cook his meals after her fashion. One day when he was partaking
of his meals in Brâhman shape at a *satra*[1], he heard the talk about the Brâhman

---

1.   A place of public feeding.

girl who was always falling in love with every beautiful Brâhman boy. Said he to himself, "Praised be the face that I saw first this morning. I shall assume the shape of a Brâhman boy, and appear as beautiful as beautiful can be, and win the heart of the girl."

Next morning he accordingly became in form a great Sâstrin (proficient in the *Râmâyana*) and took his seat near the *ghât* of the sacred river of the village. Scattering holy ashes profusely over his body he opened the *Râmâyana* and began to read.

"The voice of the new Sâstrin is most enchanting. Let us go and hear him," said some women among themselves, and sat down before him to hear him expound the great book. The girl for whom the tiger had assumed this shape came in due time to bathe at the river, and as soon as she saw the new Sâstrin fell in love with him, and bothered her old mother to speak to her father about him, so as not to lose her new lover. The old woman too was delighted at the bridegroom whom fortune had thrown in her way, and ran home to her husband, who, when he came and saw the Sâstrin, raised up his hands in praise of the great god Mahêśvara. The Sâstrin was now invited to take his meals with them, and as he had come with the express intention of marrying the daughter he, of course, agreed.

A grand dinner followed in honour of the Sâstrin, and his host began to question him as to his parentage, &c., to which the cunning tiger replied that he was born in a village beyond the adjacent wood. The Brâhman had no time to wait for better enquiry, and as the boy was very fair he married his daughter to him the very next day. Feasts followed for a month, during which time the bridegroom gave every satisfaction to his new relatives, who supposed him to be human all the while. He also did full justice to the Brâhmanic dishes, and gorged everything that was placed before him.

After the first month was over the tiger-bridegroom bethought him of his accustomed prey, and hankered after his abode in the woods. A change of diet for a day or two is all very well, but to renounce his own proper food for more than a month was hard. So one day he said to his father-in-law, "I must go back soon to my old parents, for they will be pining at my absence. But why should we have to bear the double expense of my coming all the way here again to take my wife to my village? So if you will kindly let me take the girl with me I shall take her to her future home, and hand her over to her mother-in-law, and see that she is well taken care of." The old Brâhmaṇ agreed to this, and replied, "My dear son-in-law, you are her husband and she is yours and we now send her with you, though it is like sending her into the wilderness with her eyes tied up. But as we take you to be everything to her, we trust you to treat her kindly." The mother of the bride shed tears at the idea of having to send her away, but nevertheless the very next day was fixed for the journey. The old woman spent the whole day in preparing cakes and sweetmeats for her daughter, and when the time for the journey arrived, she took care to place in her bundles and on her head one or two margosa[2] leaves to keep off demons. The relatives of the bride requested her husband to allow her to rest wherever she found shade, and to eat wherever she found water, and to this he agreed, and so they began their journey.

The boy tiger and his human wife pursued their journey for two or three *ghaṭikâs*[3] in free and pleasant conversation, when the girl happened to see a fine pond, round which the birds were warbling their sweet notes. She requested her husband to follow her to the water's edge and to partake of some of the cakes and sweetmeats with her. But he replied, "Be quiet, or I shall show you my original shape." This made her afraid, so she pursued her journey in silence until she saw another pond, when she asked the same

---

2. Among high caste Hindûs when girls leave one village and go to another the old woman of the house—the mother or grandmother—always places in her bundles and on her head a few margosa leaves as a talisman against demons.

3. A *ghaṭikâ* is 24 minutes. The story being Hindû, the Hindû method of reckoning distance is used.

question of her husband, who replied in the same tone. Now she was very hungry, and not liking her husband's tone, which she found had greatly changed ever since they had entered the woods, said to him, "Show me your original shape."

No sooner were these words uttered than her husband remained no longer a man. Four legs, a striped skin, a long tail and a tiger's face came over him suddenly and, horror of horrors! a tiger and not a man stood before her! Nor were her fears stilled when the tiger in human voice began as follows:—"Know henceforth that I, your husband, am a tiger—this very tiger that now speaks to you. If you have any regard for your life you must obey all my orders implicitly, for I can speak to you in human voice and understand what you say. In a couple of *ghatikâs* we shall reach my home, of which you will become the mistress. In the front of my house you will see half a dozen tubs, each of which you must fill up daily with some dish or other cooked in your own way. I shall take care to supply you with all the provisions you want." So saying the tiger slowly conducted her to his house.

The misery of the girl may more be imagined than described, for if she were to object she would be put to death. So, weeping all the way, she reached her husband's house. Leaving her there he went out and returned with several pumpkins and some flesh, of which she soon prepared a curry and gave it to her husband. He went out again after this and returned in the evening with several vegetables and some more flesh and gave her an order:—"Every morning I shall go out in search of provisions and prey and bring something with me on my return: you must keep cooked for me whatever I leave in the house."

Next morning as soon as the tiger had gone away she cooked everything left in the house and filled all the tubs with food. At the 10ᵗʰ *ghatikâ* the tiger returned and growled out, "I smell a man! I smell a woman in my wood." And his wife for very fear shut herself up in the house. As soon as the tiger had satisfied his appetite he told her to open the door, which she did, and they talked together for a time, after which the tiger rested awhile, and then went out hunting again. Thus passed many a day, till the tiger's Brâhmaṇ wife had a son, which also turned out to be only a tiger.

One day, after the tiger had gone out to the woods, his wife was crying all alone in the house, when a crow happened to peck at some rice that was scattered near her, and seeing the girl crying, began to shed tears.

"Can you assist me?" asked the girl.

"Yes," said the crow.

So she brought out a palmyra leaf and wrote on it with an iron nail all her sufferings in the wood, and requested her brothers to come and relieve her. This palmyra leaf she tied to the neck of the crow, which, seeming to understand her thoughts, flew to her village and sat down before one of her brothers. He untied the leaf and read the contents of the letter and told them to his other brothers. All the three then started for the wood, asking their mother to give them something to eat on the way. She had not enough of rice for the three, so she made a big ball of clay and stuck it over with what rice she had, so as to make it look like a ball of rice. This she gave to the brothers to eat on their way and started them off to the woods.

They had not proceeded long before they espied an ass. The youngest, who was of a playful disposition, wished to take the ass with him. The two elder brothers objected to this for a time, but in the end they allowed him to have his own way. Further on they saw an ant, which the middle brother took with him. Near the ant there was a big palmyra tree lying on the ground, which the eldest took with him to keep off the tiger.

The sun was now high in the horizon and the three brothers became very hungry. So they sat down near a tank and opened the bundle containing the ball of rice. To their utter disappointment they found it to be all clay, but being extremely hungry they drank all the water in the pond and continued their journey. On leaving the tank they found a big iron tub belonging to the washerman of the adjacent village. This they took also with them in addition to the ass, the ant and the palmyra tree. Following the road described by their sister in her letter by the crow, they walked on and on till they reached the tiger's house.

The sister, overjoyed to see her brothers again, ran out at once to welcome them. "My dearest brothers, I am so glad to see that you have come here to relieve me after all, but the time for the tiger's coming home is approaching, so hide yourselves in the loft, and wait till he is gone." So saying she helped her brothers to ascend into the loft. By this time the tiger returned, and perceived the presence of human beings by the peculiar smell. He asked his wife whether any one had come to their house. She said, "No." But when the brothers, who with their trophies of the way—the ass, the ant, and so on—were sitting upon the loft, saw the tiger dallying with their sister they were greatly frightened; so much so that the youngest through fear began to make water, and, as he had drunk a great quantity of water from the pond, he flooded the whole room. The other two also followed his example, and thus there was a deluge in the tiger's house.

"What is all this?" said the terrified tiger to his wife.

"Nothing," said she, "but the urine of your brothers-in-law. They came here a watch[4] ago, and as soon as you have finished your meals, they want to see you."

"Can my brothers-in-law make all this water?" thought the tiger to himself.

He then asked them to speak to him, whereon the youngest brother put the ant which he had in his hand into the ear of the ass, and as soon as the latter was bitten, it began to bawl out most horribly.

"How is it that your brothers have such a hoarse voice?" said the tiger to his wife.

---

4.   A "watch" is a *yâma*, or three hours.

He next asked them to show their legs. Taking courage at the stupidity of the tiger on the two former occasions, the eldest brother now stretched out the palmyra tree.

"By my father, I have never seen such a leg," said the tiger, and asked his brothers-in-law to show their bellies. The second brother now showed the tub, at which the tiger shuddered, and saying, "such a lot of urine, such a harsh voice, so stout a leg and such a belly, truly I have never heard of such persons as these!" he ran away.

It was already dark, and the brothers, wishing to take advantage of the tiger's terror, prepared to return home with their sister at once. They ate up what little food she had, and ordered her to start. Fortunately for her her tiger-child was asleep. So she tore it into two pieces and suspended them over the hearth, and, thus getting rid of the child, she ran off with her brothers towards home.

Before leaving she bolted the front door from inside, and went out at the back of the house. As soon as the pieces of the cub, which were hung up over the hearth, began to roast they dripped, which made the fire hiss and sputter; and when the tiger returned at about midnight, he found the door shut and heard the hissing of the fire, which he mistook for the noise of cooking muffins.[5]

"I see!" said he to himself, "how very cunning you are! you have bolted the door and are cooking muffins for your brothers! Let us see if we can't get your muffins." So saying he went round to the back door and entered his house, and was greatly perplexed to find his cub torn in two and being roasted, his house deserted by his Brâhmaṇ wife, and his property plundered! For his wife, before leaving, had taken with her as much of the tiger's property as she could conveniently carry.

The tiger now discovered all the treachery of his wife, and his heart grieved for the loss of his son, that was now no more. He determined to

---

5. Tamil, *tôsai.*

be revenged on his wife, and to bring her back into the wood, and there tear her into many pieces in place of only two. But how to bring her back? He assumed his original shape of a young bridegroom, making, of course, due allowance for the number of years that had passed since his marriage, and the next morning went to his father-in-law's house. His brothers-in-law and his wife saw from a distance the deceitful form he had assumed and devised means to kill him. Meanwhile the tiger Brâhman approached his father-in-law's house, and the old people welcomed him. The younger ones too ran here and there to bring provisions to feed him sumptuously, and the tiger was highly pleased at the hospitable way in which he was received.

There was a ruined well at the back of the house, and the eldest of the brothers placed some thin sticks across its mouth, over which he spread a fine mat. Now it is usual to ask guests to have an oil bath before dinner, and so his three brothers-in-law requested the tiger to take his seat on the fine mat for his bath. As soon as he sat on it the thin sticks being unable to bear his weight gave way and down fell the cunning tiger with a heavy crash! The well was at once filled in with stones and other rubbish, and thus the tiger was effectually prevented from doing any more mischief.

But the Brâhman girl, in memory of her having married a tiger, raised a pillar over the well and planted a *tulasî* [6] shrub on the top of it. Morning and evening, for the rest of her life, she used to smear the pillar with sacred cow-dung and water the *tulasî* shrub.

This story is told to explain the Tamiḻ proverb *"Śummâ irukkiraya, śuruvattai kâṭṭaṭṭuma,"* which means—

"Be quiet, or I shall show you my original shape."

---

6.   A fragrant herb, held in great veneration by the Hindûs; *Ocymum sanctum*. This herb is sacred alike to Śiva and Vishṇu. Those species specially sacred to Śiva are—*Vendulasî; Śiru-tulasî*, and *Śiva-tulasî*; those to Vishṇu are *Śendulasî, Karundulasî*, and *Vishṇu-tulasî*.

THE SOOTHSAYER'S SON

❖ ⋯❖⋯ ❖

Tamil Nadu

जन्ममभृति दारिद्र्यं दशवर्षाणि बन्धनम् ।
समुद्रतीरे मरणं किञ्चित् भोगं भविष्यति ॥

Thus a Soothsayer when on his death-bed wrote the horoscope of his second son, and bequeathed it to him as his only property, leaving the whole of his estate to his eldest son. The second son pondered over the horoscope, and fell into the following contemplations:—

"Alas, am I born to this only in the world? The sayings of my father never failed. I have seen them prove true to the last word while he was living; and how has he fixed my horoscope! *Janma prabhṛiti dâridryam!* From my birth poverty! I am not to be in that miserable condition alone. *Daśa varshâṇi bandhanam*: for ten years, imprisonment—a fate harder than poverty; and what comes next? *Samudratîrê maraṇam*: death on the sea-shore; which means that I must die away from home, far from friends and relatives on a sea-coast. The misery has reached its extreme height here. Now comes the funniest part of the horoscope. *Kiñchit bhôgaṁ bhavishyati*—that I am to have some happiness afterwards! What this happiness is, is an enigma to me: to die first, to be happy for some time after! What happiness? Is it the happiness of this world? So it must be. For however clever one may be, he cannot foretell what may take place in the other world. Therefore it must be the happiness of this world; and how can that be possible after my death? It is impossible. I think my father has only meant this as a consoling conclusion to the series of calamities that he has prophesied. Three portions of his prophecy must prove true; the fourth and last is a mere comforting statement to bear patiently the calamitites enumerated, and never to prove true. Therefore let me go to Bânâras, bathe in the holy Gaṅgâ, wash away my sins, and prepare myself for my end. Let me avoid sea-coasts, lest death meet me there in accordance with my father's words. Come imprisonment: I am prepared for it for ten years."

Thus thought he, and after all the funeral obsequies of his father were over, took leave of his elder brother, and started for Bânâras. He went by the middle of the Dakhaṇ, avoiding both the coasts, and went on journeying and journeying for weeks and months, till at last he reached the Vindhya mountains. While passing that desert he had to journey for a couple of days through a sandy plain, with no signs of life or vegetation. The little store of provision with which he was provided for a couple of days, at last was exhausted. The *chombu*, which he carried always full, replenishing it with the sweet water from the flowing rivulet or plenteous tank, he had exhausted in the heat of the desert. There was not a morsel in his hand to eat; nor a drop of water to drink. Turn his eyes wherever he might he found a vast desert, out of which he saw no means of escape. Still he thought within himself, "Surely my father's prophecy never proved untrue. I must survive this calamity to find my death on some sea-coast." So thought he, and this thought gave him strength of mind to walk fast and try to find a drop of water somewhere to slake his dry throat. At last he succeeded, or rather thought that he succeeded. Heaven threw in his way a ruined well. He thought that he could collect some water if he let down his *chombu* with the string that he always carried noosed to the neck of it. Accordingly he let it down; it went some way and stopped, and the following words came from the well, "Oh, relieve me! I am the king of tigers, dying here of hunger. For the last three days I have had nothing. Fortune has sent you here. If you assist me now you will find a sure help in me throughout your life. Do not think that I am a beast of prey. When you have become my deliverer I can never touch you. Pray kindly lift me up." Gaṅgâdhara, for that was the name of the Soothsayer's second son, found himself in a very perplexing position. "Shall I take him out or not? If I take him out he may make me the first morsel of his hungry mouth. No; that he will not do. For my father's prophecy never came untrue. I must die on a sea-coast and not by a tiger." Thus thinking, he asked the tiger-king to hold tight the vessel, which he accordingly did, and he lifted him up slowly. The tiger reached the top of the well and felt himself on safe ground. True to his word he did no harm to Gaṅgâdhara. On the other hand, he went round his patron three times, and standing before him, humbly spoke the following words:—"My life-giver, my benefactor! I shall never forget this day, when I regained my life through your kind hands. In return for this kind assistance I pledge my oath to stand by you in all calamities. Whenever you are in any difficulty just think of me. I am there with you ready to oblige you by all the means that I can. To tell you briefly how I came in here:—Three days ago I was roaming in yonder forest, when I saw a goldsmith passing through it. I chased him. He, finding it impossible to escape my claws, jumped into this well, and is living to this moment in the very bottom of it. I also jumped, but found myself in the first storey; he is on the last and fourth storey. In the second storey lives a serpent half-famished with hunger. In the third storey lies a rat, similarly half-famished, and when you again begin to draw water these may request you first to release them. In the same way the goldsmith also may request. I tell you, as your bosom friend, never assist that wretched man, though he is your relation as a human being. Goldsmiths are never to be trusted. You can place more faith in me, a tiger, though I feast sometimes upon men, in a serpent whose sting makes your blood cold the very next moment, or in a rat, which does a thousand mischiefs in your house. But never trust a goldsmith. Do not release him; and if you do, you shall surely repent of it one day or other." Thus advising, the hungry tiger went away without waiting for an answer.

Gangâdhara thought several times of the eloquent way in which the tiger addressed him, and admired his fluency of speech. His thirst was not quenched. So he let down his vessel again, which was now caught hold of by the serpent, who addressed him thus:—"Oh my protector! lift me up. I am the king of serpents, and the son of Âdisêsha, who is now pining away in agony for my disappearance. Release me now. I shall ever remain your servant, remember your assistance, and help you throughout life in all possible ways. Oblige me: I am dying." Gangâdhara, calling again to mind the *Samudratîrê maranam*—death on the seashore—lifted him up. He, like the tiger-king, circumambulated him thrice, and prostrating himself before him spoke thus:—"Oh, my life-giver, my father, for so I must call you, as you have given me another birth, I have already told you that I am Âdisê-sha's son, and that I am the king of the serpents. I was three days ago basking myself in the morning sun, when I saw a rat running before me. I chased it. He fell into this well. I followed him, but instead of falling on the third storey where he is now lying, I fell into the second. It was on the same evening that the goldsmith also fell down on the fourth storey, and the tiger whom you released just before me fell down into the first. What I have to tell you now is—do not relieve the goldsmith, though you may release the rat. As a rule, goldsmiths are never to be trusted. I am going away now to see my father. Whenever you are in any difficulty just think of me. I will be there by your side to assist you by all possible means. If, not-withstanding my repeated advice, you happen to release the goldsmith, you shall suffer for it severely." So saying, the Nâgarâja (serpent-king) glided away in zigzag movements, and was out of sight in a moment.

The poor son of the Soothsayer who was now almost dying of thirst, and was even led to think that the messengers of death were near him, notwithstanding his firm belief in the words of his father, let down his vessel for a third time. The rat caught hold of it, and without discussing, he lifted up the poor animal at once. But it would not go without showing its eloquence—"Oh life of my life, my benefactor: I am the king of rats. Whenever you are in any calamity just think of me. I will come to you, and assist you. My keen ears overheard all that the tiger-king and the serpent-king told you about the Svarṇataskara (*gold-smith*), who is in the fourth storey. It is nothing but a sad truth that goldsmiths ought never to be trusted. Therefore never assist him as you have done to us all. And if you do you shall feel it. I am hungry; let me go for the present." Thus taking leave of his benefactor, the rat, too, ran away.

Gaṅgâdhara for a while thought upon the repeated advice given by the three animals about releasing the goldsmith, "What wrong would there be in my assisting him. Why should I not release him also." So thinking to himself Gaṅgâdhara let down the vessel again. The goldsmith caught hold of it, and demanded help. The Soothsayer's son had no time to lose; he was himself dying of thirst. Therefore he lifted the goldsmith up, who now began his story:—"Stop for a while," said Gaṅgâdhara, and after quenching his thirst by letting down his vessel for the fifth time, still fearing that some one might remain in the well and demand his assistance, he listened to the goldsmith, who began as follows:—"My dear friend, my protector, what a deal of nonsense these brutes were talking to you about me; I am glad you have not followed their advice. I am just now dying of hunger. Permit me to go away. My name is Mâṇikkâśâri. I live in the East main street of Ujjaini, which is 20 *kôs* to the south of this place, and so lies on your way when you return from Bânâras. Do not forget to come to me and receive my kind remembrances of your assistance, on your way back to your country." So saying the goldsmith took his leave, and Gaṅgâdhara also pursued his way north after the above adventures.

He reached Bânâras, and lived there for more than ten years, spending his time in bathing, prayers, and other religious ceremonies. He quite forgot the tiger, serpent, rat, and goldsmith. After ten years of religious life, thoughts of home and of his brother rushed into his mind. "Enough of the merit that I have secured till now by my religious observances. Let me return home." Thus thought Gaṅgâdhara within himself, and immediately he was on his way back to his country. Remembering the prophecy of his father he returned by the same way by which he went to Bânâras ten years before. While thus retracing his steps he reached that ruined well where he released the three brute kings and the goldsmith. At once the old recollections rushed into his mind, and he thought of the tiger to test his fidelity. Only a moment passed, and the tiger-king came running before him carrying a large crown in his mouth, the glitter of the diamonds of which for a time outshone even the bright rays of the sun. He dropped the crown at his life-giver's feet, and leaving off all his pride, humbled himself like a pet cat to the strokes of his protector, and began in the following words:—"My life-giver! How is it that you forgot me, your poor servant, for so long a time. I am glad to find that I still occupy a corner in your mind. I can never forget the day when I owed my life to your lotus hands. I have several jewels with me of little value. This crown, being the best of all, I have brought here as a single ornament of great value, and hence easily portable and useful to you in your own country." Gaṅgâdhara looked at the crown, examined it over and over, counted and recounted the gems, and thought within himself that he would become the richest of men by separating the diamonds and gold, and selling them in his own country. He took leave of the tiger-king, and after his disappearance thought of the kings of serpents and rats, who came in their turns with their presents, and after the usual formalities and exchange of words took their leave. Gaṅgâdhara was extremely delighted at the faithfulness with which the brute beasts behaved themselves, and went on his way to the south. While going along he spoke to himself thus:—"These beasts have been so very faithful in their assistance. Much more, therefore, must Mâṇikkâśâri be faithful. I do not want anything from him now. If I take this crown with me as it is, it occupies much space in my bundle. It may also excite the curiosity of some robbers on the way. I will go now to Ujjaini on my way. Mâṇikkâśâri requested me to see him without failure on my return-journey. I shall do so, and request him to have the crown melted, the diamonds and gold separated. He must do that kindness at least for me. I shall then roll up these diamonds and gold ball in my rags, and bend my way home." Thus thinking and thinking he reached Ujjaini. At once he enquired for the house of his goldsmith friend, and found him without difficulty. Mâṇikkâśâri was extremely delighted to find on his threshold him who ten years before, notwithstanding the advice repeatedly given him by the sage-looking tiger, serpent, and rat, had relieved him from the pit of death. Gaṅgâdhara at once showed him the crown that he received from the tiger-king, told him how he got it, and requested his kind assistance to separate the gold and diamonds. Mâṇikkâśâri agreed to do so, and meanwhile asked his friend to rest himself for a while to have his bath and meals; and Gaṅgâdhara, who was very observant of his religious ceremonies, went direct to the river to bathe.

How came a crown in the jaws of a tiger? It is not a difficult question to solve. A king must have furnished the table of the tiger for a day or two. Had it not been for that, the tiger could not have had a crown with him. Even so it was. The king of Ujjaini had a week before gone with all his hunters on a hunting expedition. All on a sudden a tiger—as we know now, the very tiger-king himself—started from the wood, seized the king, and vanished. The hunters returned and informed the prince about the sad calamity that had befallen his father. They all saw the tiger carrying away the king. Yet such was their courage that they could not lift their weapons to bring to the prince the corpse at least of his father; their courage reminds us of the couplet in the *Child's Story*:—

"Four and twenty sailors went to kill a snail;

The best man among them dares not touch her tail."

When they informed the prince about the death of his father he wept and wailed, and gave notice that he would give half of his kingdom to any one who should bring him news about the murderer of his father. The prince did not at all believe that his father was devoured by the tiger. His belief was that some hunters, coveting the ornaments on the king's person, had murdered him. Hence he had issued the notice. The goldsmith knew full well that it was a tiger that killed the king, and not any hunter's hands, since he had heard from Gaṅgâdhara about how he obtained the crown. Still, ambition to get half the kingdom prevailed, and he resolved with himself to make over Gaṅgâdhara as the king's murderer. The crown was lying on the floor where Gaṅgâdhara left it with his full confidence in Mâṇikkâśâri. Before his protector's return the goldsmith, hiding the crown under his garments, flies to the palace. He went before the prince and informed him that the assassin was caught, and placed the crown before him. The prince took it into his hands, examined it, and at once gave half the kingdom to Mâṇikkâśâri, and then enquired about the murderer. He is bathing in the river, and is of such and such appearance, was the reply. At once four armed soldiers fly to the river, and bind hand and foot the poor Brâhmaṇ, who sits in meditation, without any knowledge of the fate that hangs over him. They brought Gaṅgâdhara to the presence of the prince, who turned his face away from the murderer or supposed murderer, and asked his soldiers to throw him into the *kârâgṛiham*. In a minute, without knowing the cause, the poor Brâhmaṇ found himself in the dark caves of the *kârâgṛiham*.

In old times the *kârâgṛiham* answered the purposes of the modern jail. It was a dark cellar underground, built with strong stone walls, into which any criminal guilty of a capital offence was ushered to breathe his last there without food and drink. Into such a cellar Gaṅgâdhara was pushed down.

In a few hours after he left the goldsmith he found himself inside a dark cell stinking with human bodies, dying and dead. What were his thoughts when he reached that place? "It is the goldsmith that has brought me to this wretched state; and, as for the prince: Why should he not enquire as to how I obtained the crown? It is of no use to accuse either the goldsmith or the prince now. We are all the children of fate. We must obey her commands. *Daśa-varshâṇi bandhanam*. This is but the first day of my father's prophecy. So far his statement is true. But how am I going to pass ten years here? Perhaps without anything to keep up my life I may drag on my existence for a day or two. But how to pass ten years? That cannot be, and I must die. Before death comes let me think of my faithful brute friends."

So pondered Gaṅgâdhara in the dark cell underground, and at that moment thought of his three friends. The tiger-king, serpent-king, and rat-king assembled at once with their armies at a garden near the *kârâgriham*, and for a while did not know what to do. A common cause—how to reach their protector who was now in the dark cell underneath—united them all. They held their council, and decided to make an underground passage from the inside of a ruined well to the *kârâgriham*. The rat *râja* issued an order at once to that effect to his army. They with their nimble teeth bored the ground a long way to the walls of the prison. After reaching it they found that their teeth could not work on the hard stones. The bandicoots were then specially ordered for the business, they with their hard teeth made a small slit in the wall for a rat to pass and repass without difficulty. Thus a passage was effected.

The rat *râja* entered first to condole with his protector for his calamity. The king of the tigers sent word through the snake-king that he sympathised most sincerely with his sorrow, and that he was ready to render all help for his deliverance. He suggested a means for his escape also. The serpent *râja* went in, and gave Gaṅgâdhara hopes of delivery. The rat king undertook to supply his protector with provisions. "Whatever sweetmeats or bread are prepared in any house, one and all of you must try to bring whatever you can to our benefactor. Whatever clothes you find hanging in a house, cut down, dip the pieces in water and bring the wet bits to our benefactor. He will squeeze them and gather water for drink; and the bread and sweetmeats shall form his food." Thus ordered the king of the rats, and took leave of Gaṅgâdhara. They in obedience to their king's order continued to supply provisions and water.

The Nâgarâja said:—"I sincerely condole with you in your calamity; the tiger-king also fully sympathises with you, and wants me to tell you so, as he cannot drag his huge body here as we have done with our small ones. The king of the rats has promised to do his best to keep up your life. We would now do what we can for your release. From this day we shall issue orders to our armies to oppress all the subjects of this kingdom. The percentage of death by snake-bite and tigers shall increase from this day. And day by day it shall continue to increase till your release. After eating what the rats bring you you had better take your seat near the entrance of the *kârâgriham*. Owing to the several unnatural deaths some people that walk over the prison might say, 'How unjust the king has turned out now. Were it not for his injustice such early deaths by snake-bite could never occur.' Whenever you hear people speaking so, you had better bawl out so as to be heard by them, 'The wretched prince imprisoned me on the false charge of having killed his father, while it was a tiger that killed him. From that day these calamities have broken out in his dominions. If I were released I would save all by my powers of healing poisonous wounds and by incantations.' Some one may report this to the king, and if he knows it, you will obtain your liberty." Thus comforting his protector in trouble, he advised him to pluck up courage, and took leave of him. From that day tigers and serpents, acting under the special orders of their kings, united in killing as many persons and cattle as possible. Every day people were being carried away by tigers or bitten by serpents. This havoc continued. Gaṅgâdhara was roaring as loud as he could that he would save those lives, had he only his liberty. Few heard him. The few that did took his words for the voice of a ghost. "How could he manage to live without food and drink for so long a time?" said the persons walking over his head to each other. Thus passed on months and years. Gaṅgâdhara sat in the dark cellar, without the sun's light falling upon him, and feasted upon the bread-crumbs and sweetmeats that the rats so kindly supplied him with. These circumstances had completely changed his body. He had become a red, stout, huge, unwieldy lump of flesh. Thus passed full ten years, as prophesied in the horoscope— *Daśa-varshâṇi bandhanam.*

Ten complete years rolled away in close imprisonment. On the last evening of the tenth year one of the serpents got into the bed-chamber of the princess and sucked her life. She breathed her last. She was the only daughter of the king. He had no other issue—son or daughter. His only hope was in her; and she was snatched away by a cruel and untimely death. The king at once sent for all the snake-bite curers. He promised half his kingdom, and his daughter's hand to him who would restore her to life. Now it was that a servant of the king who had several times overheard Gaṅgâdhara's exclamation reported the matter to him. The king at once ordered the cell to be examined. There was the man sitting in it. How has he managed to live so long in the cell? Some whispered that he must be a divine being. Some concluded that he must surely win the hand of the princess by restoring her to life. Thus they discussed and the discussions brought Gaṅgâdhara to the king.

The king no sooner saw Gaṅgâdhara than he fell on the ground. He was struck by the majesty and grandeur of his person. His ten years' imprisonment in the deep cell underground had given a sort of lustre to his body, which was not to be met with in ordinary persons. His hair had first to be cut before his face could be seen. The king begged forgiveness for his former fault, and requested him to revive his daughter.

"Bring me in a *muhûrta* all the corpses of men and cattle dying and dead, that remain unburnt or unburied within the range of your dominions; I shall revive them all:" were the only words that Gaṅgâdhara spoke. After it he closed his lips as if in deep meditation, which commanded him more respect in the company.

Cart-loads of corpses of men and cattle began to come in every minute. Even graves, it is said, were broken open, and corpses buried a day or two before were taken out and sent for the revival. As soon as all were ready Gaṅgâdhara took a vessel full of water and sprinkled it over them all, thinking upon his Nâgarâja and Vyâghrarâja. All rose up as if from deep slumber, and went to their respective homes. The princess, too, was restored to life. The joy of the king knows no bounds. He curses the day on which he imprisoned him, accuses himself for having believed the word of a goldsmith, and offers him the hand of his daughter and the whole kingdom, instead of half as he promised. Gaṅgâdhara would not accept anything. The king requested him to put a stop for ever to those calamities. He agreed to do so, and asked the king to assemble all his subjects in a wood near the town. "I shall there call in all the tigers and serpents and give them a general order." So said Gaṅgâdhara, and the king accordingly gave the order. In a couple of *ghaṭikas* the wood near Ujjaini was full of people who assembled to witness the authority of man over such enemies of human beings as tigers and serpents. "He is no man; be sure of that. How could he have managed to live for ten years without food and drink? He is surely a god." Thus speculated the mob.

When the whole town was assembled just at the dusk of evening, Gaṅgâdhara sat dumb for a moment and thought upon the Vyâghrarâja and Nâgarâja, who came running with all their armies. People began to take to their heels at the sight of the tigers. Gaṅgâdhara assured them of safety, and stopped them.

The grey light of the evening, the pumpkin colour of Gaṅgâdhara, the holy ashes scattered lavishly over his body, the tigers and snakes humbling themselves at his feet, gave him the true majesty of the god Gaṅgâdhara. For who else by a single word could thus command vast armies of tigers and serpents, said some among the people. "Care not for it; it may be by magic. That is not a great thing. That he revived cart-loads of corpses makes him surely Gaṅgâdhara," said others. The scene produced a very great effect upon the minds of the mob.

"Why should you, my children, thus trouble these poor subjects of Ujjaini? Reply to me, and henceforth desist from your ravages." Thus said the Soothsayer's son, and the following reply came from the king of the tigers; "Why should this base king imprison your honour, believing the mere word of a goldsmith that your honour killed his father? All the hunters told him that his father was carried away by a tiger. I was the messenger of death sent to deal the blow on his neck. I did it, and gave the crown to your honour. The prince makes no enquiry, and at once imprisons your honour. How can we expect justice from such a stupid king as that. Unless he adopts a better standard of justice we will go on with our destruction."

The king heard, cursed the day on which he believed in the word of the goldsmith, beat his head, tore his hair, wept and wailed for his crime, asked a thousand pardons, and swore to rule in a just way from that day. The serpent-king and the tiger-king also promised to observe their oath as long as justice prevailed, and took their leave. The goldsmith fled for his life. He was caught by the soldiers of the king, and was pardoned by the generous Gaṅgâdhara, whose voice now reigned supreme. All returned to their homes.

The king again pressed Gaṅgâdhara to accept the hand of his daughter. He agreed to do so, not then, but some time afterwards. He wished to go and see his elder brother first, and then to return and marry the princess. The king agreed; and Gaṅgâdhara left the city that very day on his way home.

It so happened that unwittingly he took a wrong road, and had to pass near a sea coast. His elder brother was also on his way up to Bânâras by that very same route. They met and recognised each other, even at a distance. They flew into each other's arms. Both remained still for a time without knowing anything. The emotion of pleasure *(ânanda)* was so great, especially in Gaṅgâdhara, that it proved dangerous to his life. In a word, he died of joy.

The sorrow of the elder brother could better be imagined than described. He saw again his lost brother, after having given up, as it were, all hopes of meeting him. He had not even asked him his adventures. That he should be snatched away by the cruel hand of death seemed unbearable to him. He wept and wailed, took the corpse on his lap, sat under a tree, and wetted it with tears. But there was no hope of his dead brother coming to life again.

The elder brother was a devout worshipper of Gaṇapati. That was a Friday, a day very sacred to that god. The elder brother took the corpse to the nearest Gaṇêśa temple and called upon him. The god came, and asked him what he wanted. "My poor brother is dead and gone; and this is his corpse. Kindly keep it under your charge till I finish your worship. If I leave it anywhere else the devils may snatch it away when I am absent in your worship; after finishing your *pûjâ* I shall burn him." Thus said the elder brother, and giving the corpse to the god Gaṇêśa he went to prepare himself for that deity's worship. Gaṇêśa made over the corpse to his *Gaṇas*, asking them to watch over it carefully.

So receives a spoiled child a fruit from its father, who, when he gives it the fruit asks the child to keep it safe. The child thinks within itself, "Papa will excuse me if I eat a portion of it." So saying it eats a portion, and when it finds it so sweet, it eats the whole, saying, "Come what will, what will papa do, after all, if I eat it? Perhaps give me a stroke or two on the back. Perhaps he may excuse me." In the same way these *Gaṇas* of Gaṇapati first ate a portion of the corpse, and when they found it sweet, for we know that it was crammed up with the sweetmeats of the kind rats, devoured the whole, and were consulting about offering the best excuse possible to their master.

The elder brother, after finishing the *pûjâ*, demanded from the god his brother's corpse. The belly-god called his *Gaṇas*, who came to the front blinking, and fearing the anger of their master. The god was greatly enraged. The elder brother was highly vexed. When the corpse was not forthcoming he cuttingly remarked, "Is this, after all, the return for my deep belief in you? You are unable even to return my brother's corpse." Gaṇêśa was much ashamed at the remark, and at the uneasiness that he had caused to his worshipper, so he by his divine power gave him a living Gaṅgâdhara instead of the dead corpse. Thus was the second son of the Soothsayer restored to life.

The brothers had a long talk about each other's adventures. They both went to Ujjaini, where Gaṅgâdhara married the princess, and succeeded to the throne of that kingdom. He reigned for a long time, conferring several benefits upon his brother. How is the horoscope to be interpreted? A special synod of Soothsayers was held. A thousand emendations were suggested. Gaṅgâdhara would not accept them. At last one Soothsayer cut the knot by stopping at a different place in reading, "*Samudratîrê maraṇam kiñchit.*" "On the sea shore death for some time. Then *Bhôgam bhavishyati.* There shall be happiness for the person concerned." Thus the passage was interpreted. "Yes; my father's words never went wrong," said Gaṅgâdhara. The three brute kings continued their visits often to the Soothsayer's son, the then king of Ujjaini. Even the faithless goldsmith became a frequent visitor at the palace, and a receiver of several benefits from the royal hands.

THE RAT'S WEDDING

Punjab

Once upon a time a fat sleek Rat was caught in a shower of rain, and being far from shelter he set to work and soon dug a nice hole in the ground, in which he sat as dry as a bone while the raindrops splashed outside, making little puddles on the road.

Now in the course of his digging he came upon a fine bit of root, quite dry and fit for fuel, which he set aside carefully—for the Rat is an economical creature—in order to take it home with him. So when the shower was over, he set off with the dry root in his mouth. As he went along, daintily picking his way through the puddles, he saw a poor man vainly trying to light a fire, while a little circle of children stood by, and cried piteously.

"Goodness gracious!" exclaimed the Rat, who was both soft-hearted and curious, "what a dreadful noise to make! What *is* the matter?"

"The bairns are hungry," answered the man; "they are crying for their breakfast, but the sticks are damp, the fire won't burn, and so I can't bake the cakes."

"If that is all your trouble, perhaps I can help you," said the good-natured Rat; "you are welcome to this dry root, and I'll warrant it will soon make a fine blaze."

The poor man, with a thousand thanks, took the dry root, and in his turn presented the Rat with a morsel of dough, as a reward for his kindness and generosity.

"What a remarkably lucky fellow I am!" thought the Rat, as he trotted off gaily with his prize, "and clever too! Fancy making a bargain like that—food enough to last me five days in return for a rotten old stick! *Wah! wah! wah!* what it is to have brains!"

Going along, hugging his good fortune in this way, he came presently to a potter's yard, where the potter, leaving his wheel to spin round by itself, was trying to pacify his three little children, who were screaming and crying as if they would burst.

"My gracious!" cried the Rat, stopping his ears, "what a noise!—do tell me what it is all about."

"I suppose they are hungry," replied the potter ruefully; "their mother has gone to get flour in the bazaar, for there is none in the house. In the meantime I can neither work nor rest because of them."

"Is that all!" answered the officious Rat; "then I can help you. Take this dough, cook it quickly, and stop their mouths with food."

The potter overwhelmed the Rat with thanks for his obliging kindness, and choosing out a nice well-burnt pipkin, insisted on his accepting it as a remembrance.

The Rat was delighted at the exchange, and though the pipkin was just a trifle awkward for him to manage, he succeeded after infinite trouble in balancing it on his head, and went away gingerly, *tink-a-tink*, *tink-a-tink*, down the road, with his tail over his arm for fear he should trip on it. And all the time he kept saying to himself, "What a lucky fellow I am! and clever too! Such a hand at a bargain!"

By and by he came to where some neatherds were herding their cattle. One of them was milking a buffalo, and having no pail he used his shoes instead.

"Oh fie! oh fie!" cried the cleanly Rat, quite shocked at the sight. "What a nasty dirty trick!—why don't you use a pail?"

"For the best of all reasons—we haven't got one!" growled the neatherd, who did not see why the Rat should put his finger in the pie.

"If that is all," replied the dainty Rat, "oblige me by using this pipkin, for I cannot bear dirt!"

The neatherd, nothing loath, took the pipkin, and milked away until it was brimming over; then turning to the Rat, who stood looking on, said, "Here, little fellow, you may have a drink, in payment."

But if the Rat was good-natured he was also shrewd. "No, no, my friend," said he, "that will not do! As if I could drink the worth of my pipkin at a draught! My dear sir, *I couldn't hold it!* Besides, I never make a bad bargain, so I expect you at least to give me the buffalo that gave the milk."

"Nonsense!" cried the neatherd; "a buffalo for a pipkin! Who ever heard of such a price? And what on earth could *you* do with a buffalo when you got it? Why, the pipkin was about as much as you could manage."

At this the Rat drew himself up with dignity, for he did not like allusions to his size.

"That is my affair, not yours," he retorted; "your business is to hand over the buffalo."

So just for the fun of the thing, and to amuse themselves at the Rat's expense, the neatherds loosed the buffalo's halter and began to tie it to the little animal's tail.

"No! no!" he called, in a great hurry; "if the beast pulled, the skin of my tail would come off, and then where should I be? Tie it round my neck, if you please."

So with much laughter the neatherds tied the halter round the Rat's neck, and he, after a polite leave-taking, set off gaily towards home with his prize; that is to say, he set off with the *rope*, for no sooner did he come to the end of the tether than he was brought up with a round turn; the buffalo, nose down grazing away, would not budge until it had finished its tuft of grass, and then seeing another in a different direction marched off towards it, while the Rat, to avoid being dragged, had to trot humbly behind, willy-nilly.

He was too proud to confess the truth, of course, and, nodding his head knowingly to the neatherds, said, "Ta-ta, good people! I am going home this way. It may be a little longer, but it's much shadier."

And when the neatherds roared with laughter he took no notice, but trotted on, looking as dignified as possible.

"After all," he reasoned to himself, "when one keeps a buffalo one has to look after its grazing. A beast must get a good bellyful of grass if it is to give any milk, and I have plenty of time at my disposal."

So all day long he trotted about after the buffalo, making believe; but by evening he was dead tired, and felt truly thankful when the great big beast, having eaten enough, lay down under a tree to chew the cud.

Just then a bridal party came by. The bridegroom and his friends had evidently gone on to the next village, leaving the bride's palanquin to follow; so the palanquin bearers, being lazy fellows and seeing a nice shady tree, put down their burden, and began to cook some food.

"What detestable meanness!" grumbled one; "a grand wedding, and nothing but plain rice pottage to eat! Not a scrap of meat in it, neither sweet nor salt! It would serve the skinflints right if we upset the bride into a ditch!"

"Dear me!" cried the Rat at once, seeing a way out of his difficulty, "that *is* a shame! I sympathise with your feelings so entirely that if you will allow me I'll give you my buffalo. You can kill it, and cook it."

"*Your* buffalo!" returned the discontented bearers, "what rubbish! Whoever heard of a rat owning a buffalo?"

"Not often, I admit," replied the Rat with conscious pride; "but look for yourselves. Can you not see that I am leading the beast by a string?"

"Oh, never mind the string!" cried a great big hungry bearer; "master or no master, I mean to have meat to my dinner!"

Whereupon they killed the buffalo, and, cooking its flesh, ate their dinner with relish; then, offering the remains to the Rat, said carelessly, "Here, little Rat-skin, that is for you!"

"Now look here!" cried the Rat hotly; "I'll have none of your pottage, nor your sauce either. You don't suppose I am going to give my best buffalo, that gave quarts and quarts of milk—the buffalo I have been feeding all day—for a wee bit of rice? No!—I got a loaf for a bit of stick; I got a pipkin for a little loaf; I got a buffalo for a pipkin; and now I'll have the bride for my buffalo—the bride, and nothing else!"

By this time the servants, having satisfied their hunger, began to reflect on what they had done, and becoming alarmed at the consequences, arrived at the conclusion it would be wisest to make their escape whilst they could. So, leaving the bride in her palanquin, they took to their heels in various directions.

The Rat, being as it were left in possession, advanced to the palanquin, and drawing aside the curtain, with the sweetest of voices and best of bows begged the bride to descend. She hardly knew whether to laugh or to cry, but as any company, even a Rat's, was better than being quite alone in the wilderness, she did as she was bidden, and followed the lead of her guide, who set off as fast as he could for his hole.

As he trotted along beside the lovely young bride, who, by her rich dress and glittering jewels, seemed to be some king's daughter, he kept saying to himself, "How clever I am! What bargains I do make, to be sure!"

When they arrived at his hole, the Rat stepped forward with the greatest politeness, and said, "Welcome, madam, to my humble abode! Pray step in, or if you will allow me, and as the passage is somewhat dark, I will show you the way."

Whereupon he ran in first, but after a time, finding the bride did not follow, he put his nose out again, saying testily, "Well, madam, why don't you follow? Don't you know it's rude to keep your husband waiting?"

"My good sir," laughed the handsome young bride, "I can't squeeze into that little hole!"

The Rat coughed; then after a moment's thought he replied, "There is some truth in your remark—you *are* overgrown, and I suppose I shall have to build you a thatch somewhere. For to-night you can rest under that wild plum-tree."

"But I am so hungry!" said the bride ruefully.

"Dear, dear! everybody seems hungry to-day!" returned the Rat pettishly; "however, that's easily settled—I'll fetch you some supper in a trice."

So he ran into his hole, returning immediately with an ear of millet and a dry pea.

"There!" said he, triumphantly, "isn't that a fine meal?"

"I can't eat that!" whimpered the bride; "it isn't a mouthful; and I want rice pottage, and cakes, and sweet eggs, and sugar-drops. I shall die if I don't get them!"

"Oh dear me!" cried the Rat in a rage, "what a nuisance a bride is, to be sure! Why don't you eat the wild plums?"

"I can't live on wild plums!" retorted the weeping bride; "nobody could; besides, they are only half ripe, and I can't reach them."

"Rubbish!" cried the Rat; "ripe or unripe, they must do you for to-night, and to-morrow you can gather a basketful, sell them in the city, and buy sugar-drops and sweet eggs to your heart's content!"

So the next morning the Rat climbed up into the plum-tree, and nibbled away at the stalks till the fruit fell down into the bride's veil. Then, unripe as they were, she carried them into the city, calling out through the streets—

"Green plums I sell! Green plums I sell! Princess am I, Rat's bride as well!"

As she passed by the palace, her mother the Queen heard her voice, and, running out, recognised her daughter. Great were the rejoicings, for every one thought the poor bride had been eaten by wild beasts. In the midst of the feasting and merriment, the Rat, who had followed the Princess at a distance, and had become alarmed at her long absence, arrived at the door, against which he beat with a big knobby stick, calling out fiercely, "Give me my wife! give me my wife! She is mine by fair bargain. I gave a stick and I got a loaf; I gave a loaf and I got a pipkin; I gave a pipkin and I got a buffalo; I gave a buffalo and I got a bride. Give me my wife! give me my wife!"

"La! son-in-law! what a fuss you do make!" said the wily old Queen, through the door, "and all about nothing! Who wants to run away with your wife? On the contrary, we are proud to see you, and I only keep you waiting at the door till we can spread the carpets, and receive you in style."

Hearing this, the Rat was mollified, and waited patiently outside whilst the cunning old Queen prepared for his reception, which she did by cutting a hole in the very middle of a stool, putting a red-hot stone underneath, covering it over with a stewpan-lid, and then spreading a beautiful embroidered cloth over all.

Then she went to the door, and receiving the Rat with the greatest respect, led him to the stool, praying him to be seated.

"Dear! dear! how clever I am! What bargains I do make, to be sure!" said he to himself as he climbed on to the stool. "Here I am, son-in-law to a real live Queen! What will the neighbours say?"

At first he sat down on the edge of the stool, but even there it was warm, and after a while he began to fidget, saying, "Dear me, mother-in-law! how hot your house is! Everything I touch seems burning!"

"You are out of the wind there, my son," replied the cunning old Queen; "sit more in the middle of the stool, and then you will feel the breeze and get cooler."

But he didn't! for the stewpan-lid by this time had become so hot, that the Rat fairly frizzled when he sat down on it; and it was not until he had left all his tail, half his hair, and a large piece of his skin behind him, that he managed to escape, howling with pain, and vowing that never, never, never again would he make a bargain!

GHOLÂM BADSHAH
and HIS SON GHOOL

Punjab

There was once a king by name Gholâm who had an only son named Ghool. From his early years this young prince was passionately devoted to the pleasures of the field, and though now grown to manhood, his whole time was spent in hunting. The king, his father, could not behold such a condition of things as this without concern, and one day he called his ministers together and said to them: "It is time for my son to marry. Choose out a wife for him and let him settle."

The ministers, however, chose in vain. The prince continued to hunt, and though the king remonstrated with him every evening on his return from the chase, his remonstrances were all disregarded. "If you do not marry," said the king, "everyone will say it is because no one will have you, and you will suffer in reputation accordingly."

"But I do not want to marry," the prince would answer, and so the matter would remain until the next day.

One evening in the hot weather the young prince, weary with hunting, was returning home, when he stopped to rest by a well. "Let me drink from your vessel," said he to one of the damsels who were drawing water.

"Oh," answered saucily the young girl, "you are the prince whom no one will marry!"

Prince Ghool was so angry when he heard this speech that he refused to accept the water which was offered to him, and, rising, he walked away. "When I get home," said he to himself, "I shall announce my intention to marry, but my wife shall be the girl who taunted me."

Meeting an old woman, he asked of her: "Whose daughter is that?"

"She is the daughter of Alim the blacksmith," answered the woman.

"Whether a blacksmith's daughter or a king's," thought he, "it is she whom I shall marry."

That evening his father again addressed him on the subject of marriage, and joyfully learnt that his son was willing to abide by his counsel and to marry. So he summoned his ministers once more, and bade them arrange for the marriage and to choose out some suitable lady. The ministers answered: "Name the king with whose house you desire an alliance, and we will set out for his court forthwith, and the prince shall bring the bride home."

But the prince answered: "Nay, there is no need for you to look abroad. I have made my choice. I will marry Alim the blacksmith's daughter."

Then was the old king filled with anger. "What," cried he, "is my nobility to be mated with people of low degree?"

But the ministers craftily answered him: "What harm will it do? This is merely a young man's fancy. Let him have the girl, and meanwhile we will look out for another lady worthy of his rank."

The king now consented to the match, and ordered his ministers to procure the blacksmith's daughter in marriage for Prince Ghool. When they went to the house the poor man held up his hands in dismay and said: "Why does the king ask where he can command? But, indeed, as he asks for her, I am by no means willing to part with her."

This answer was reported to the king, who would brook no denial in the matter, and ordered that the blacksmith should surrender his daughter within two months. But the daughter herself, who felt that she was not fitted for such a destiny, implored her father to petition the king to grant her relief for the space of one year. The petition was granted, and the king finally agreed that the girl should enjoy her freedom for one year more.

"Alas," said she, "I am only a poor blacksmith's daughter! What shall I do in order that people may feel respect for me when I am the wife of the prince? Let me see if I cannot test the wisdom of the king's counsellors themselves." Addressing her father, she said: "The water-melons in our little garden are as yet small. I shall make some large unburnt jars, and these I shall paint and enamel, and I will lay a water-melon in each, and when the fruit is full-grown I will challenge the king's ministers to take out the fruit without breaking the jars. And then we shall see whether kings and their ministers are better or wiser than poor folk."

So the girl did as she proposed, and having made the earthen jars of unburnt clay, she painted them, and in each she laid a growing melon. When the melons were full-grown so as to fill the empty space, she sent two of the jars containing the melons to the king, and wrote a letter requesting that the ministers should be ordered to free the melons without breaking the vessels. This letter the king read to his ministers, and commanded that they should display their wisdom accordingly. But the ministers tried in vain. For two or three days they felt the melons through the narrow necks of the vessels, and examined them carefully, but they had not the sense to perceive that the jars were formed of unbaked clay, which they could easily have discovered by sounding them. At last the king sent back the jars to the daughter of the blacksmith saying: "There are no such wise people in the whole of my kingdom."

The girl was delighted beyond measure when she received this news, and when she had taken the jars into her hands she said: "I now begin to understand what kings' courtiers are, and what kings are also." Sending to the palace, she requested permission to attend, and when she entered the presence of the king, she took a wet cloth and wrapped it round the jars until the clay was quite soft. She then stretched the necks and drew forth the melons, after which she restored the jars to their former shape. Handing them to the abashed ministers, she said: "A man is known by his words, and a vessel is known by its sound. As by sounding a vessel of clay you find out its true nature, so I have sounded you, and I find you wanting in sense, and now, when the year is over, the king's commands shall be obeyed."

When the term of probation was nearly over, the blacksmith wrote to the king a petition praying that, as his means were small, the guests to be entertained in his house should be few. The king answered: "Four hundred will attend from the court, and for these only I will myself be chargeable," and he sent him a sum of money.

At last the day arrived and the guests assembled, but the blacksmith, finding the sum insufficient, said: "There is a great number of people here;" and he went to a certain nobleman and stated his difficulty. The nobleman advised him to keep the money as dower for his daughter, and to send it back with her to the king, and meanwhile he spoke to the court party, who all promised their assistance in entertaining the rest of the guests, and the feast passed off very well.

When all was over, and the prince and the girl were united in wedlock, the king's party returned to the palace, and the bride and her dower were taken home and she was lodged in the apartments reserved for her.

When two or three days had passed by, Prince Ghool rose up early one morning, and, taking a whip, he lashed his new wife unmercifully. "This is what I owe you," said he, "for your taunt to me at the well." The girl bore the beating in surprised silence. Every two or three days the same scene was enacted, the prince with his own hands baring the shoulders of his unhappy wife and ill-using her.

One morning, when he got up as usual to beat her, she said to him: "What glory do you gain by beating a poor working man's child? If you are a man, you will go and marry a king's daughter. Win her if you can, and beat her if you dare: but I am only the daughter of a blacksmith."

On hearing this taunt, the prince was so incensed that he dropped the whip and vowed never to enter the house again until he had married the daughter of a king.

Now, there was a certain princess, the daughter of a neighbouring king, whose beauty was justly celebrated, though she was said to be dumb, and she it was whom the prince determined to marry. So he chose out a trusty slave and his best horse, and, having loaded several mules with jewels and presents of inestimable value, he set out one morning for the court of the king her father. March by march he travelled along, until at last he reached the kingdom, but in answer to his inquiries all he could learn from the inhabitants was that the princess could not speak, and that every prince who came before her as a suitor had to consent to play chess with her, and that the penalties which she inflicted on his presumption when he lost the game were of the severest description. Nevertheless, Prince Ghool had so much vain confidence in his own powers that, nothing daunted, he sent forward his slave to announce his arrival to the princess, and to request the honour of her hand in marriage.

"It is necessary," answered the princess, "that your master should understand the conditions. He must try his skill with me in three games of chess. If he lose the first, he forfeits his horse; if the second, his head is to be at my mercy; and if he loses the third, it shall be my right, if I choose, to make him a groom in my stables."

The prince at once accepted these proposals, and the event was made known in the city by the sounding of a great drum. "Ah," said the people, when they heard the familiar sound, "another prince endowed with 'blind wisdom' has come to play with the princess, and he will lose, as all others have lost before him!"

When the prince arrived at the palace, he was admitted, and there he found the princess seated on a rich carpet, while the chess-board lay on the carpet in front of her. The first game he lost, and the second, and the third. "Begone, presumptuous pretender," cried she, "and take your place with your predecessors; you are only fitted to groom my horses!" So the unfortunate claimant for her hand was led away and set to mind one of her horses.

Some time had elapsed, when the blacksmith's daughter began to wonder at the continued absence of her lord, and she determined to follow him in order to learn his fate. So she disguised herself as a young nobleman, and very handsome she looked in her new attire when riding her beautiful steed. After a journey of many miles, she came to a river broad and deep, and, as she stood on the bank waiting for the ferry-boat, she observed a rat being carried down by the stream. "For God's sake," cried the drowning rat, "save me! Help me, and I will help you!"

The blacksmith's daughter said to herself: "No rat can possibly help me, yet I will certainly save you;" and she lowered the point of her lance to the water, and the rat, seizing it, climbed up to her and was saved. Taking the dripping creature in her hand, she placed it in safety on her saddle-bow.

"Where are you going?" asked the rat.

"I am going to the kingdom of the dumb princess," answered she.

"What is the use of your going there?" said the rat. "What will you gain? The princess possesses a magic cat, and on the head of the magic cat there stands a magic light which renders her invisible, and enables her to mix up all the chessmen unperceived, so that the princess's suitors invariably lose the game and are ruined."

Hearing this, the blacksmith's daughter began to fondle and pet the rat, and to say to it: "Assist me, for I also would try my fortune with the princess," while at the same time she felt that her husband had tried his fortune and had lost.

Then the rat looked at her, and said: "Your hands and your feet are those of a woman, though your dress is that of a man. First, tell me truly, are you really a man, or am I lacking in wisdom?"

Then she began to tell the creature all her history from beginning to end, and how she had set out in search of her husband, Prince Ghool. "And now," said she, "I want your assistance to recover my husband's liberty and to restore him to his rank and position."

This was a rat which never forgot a kindness, but, on the contrary, always endeavoured to repay a benefactor tenfold. "You must take me with you," said he, "hidden in your clothing, and if you will follow my advice you will beat the princess and you will attain your utmost desires." The rat then instructed her in the means of achieving a victory, and so at last in conversation of a pleasing description they approached the capital and there rested.

The next day, when the blacksmith's daughter was admitted to the princess's reception-room, she began by requesting that she might change places with her at the chess-board; and, as her request was granted, she secured the side on which the magic cat invariably entered the room. Then the game began; but soon she perceived that the board was becoming confused, and that she was gradually losing ground. Seeing this, she produced the rat, holding it the while firmly in her hand. Immediately she felt a sudden rush as of some animal, which, in fact, was the cat herself, which had that moment entered, and which in her eagerness to pounce on the rat had forgotten all about the game and her mistress's interests. The blacksmith's daughter, though she could not see the cat, still struck at her with her hand, and the magic light fell to the floor. Poor pussy was now rendered perfectly visible, and, having been scared by the unexpected blow, she ran with hair erect out of the room.

When the princess perceived these untoward occurrences, she trembled and lost heart, so that she was easily beaten, not only in the first game, but in the succeeding ones as well.

At that moment the sound of the great drum was heard reverberating through the city, and the inhabitants knew by that signal the result of the game.

Now, there was one more condition attached to the wooing of this princess, which she had the privilege of insisting upon before she could be compelled to surrender her hand. It was that her suitor should prevail upon her to speak three times before sunrise; and it was ordained by a decree that each time she spoke the great drum should be sounded by an attendant slave, for the information of all the king's subjects.

"You see," said the rat to the blacksmith's daughter, "the assistance I have rendered you has not been in vain. And now let us see if we cannot make this obstinate princess speak. Your sleeping places will not be divided even by a curtain. Keep me with you, and when you are both in bed, set me loose, and I will get on the princess's bed, while you must coax her to speak."

When they had retired and had lain down each on her own side of the apartment, the blacksmith's daughter in her feigned voice began: "Charming princess, light and glory of my eyes, will you not speak to me?"

The princess vouchsafed not a word. But the rat, which was sitting by one of the legs of her bed, imitating the princess's voice, exclaimed with the utmost tenderness: "Dear prince, sweet prince, at your request I could speak on for ever!"

When the princess heard this extraordinary statement, she thought to herself: "This prince is such a master of magic that he makes the very leg of my bed imitate my voice and answer for me." Then, shaking with rage, she cried to the inanimate wood: "To-morrow morning you shall be hacked off and burnt in the fire for disgracing your mistress."

The instant these words were uttered by her, the attendant slave ran to the tower and sounded the drum, and all the people heard and wondered. At the same time the blacksmith's daughter cried joyfully, "Salaam Alaikim, to the leg of my charmer's bed!" to which the concealed rat replied: "To you also, my king, Alaikim salaam!"

After a minute or two the blacksmith's daughter, again addressing the angry princess, said in coaxing tones: "As I have to lodge under your roof to-night, O sweet princess, pray tell me a story to send me to sleep!" The rat, having moved away to another leg of the bed, immediately answered: "Shall I tell you what I have witnessed with my own eyes, or merely something which has happened to me?"

"The best story," replied the blacksmith's daughter, "would comprise both what you have seen and what has happened to you."

"Very well," said the rat, "I will tell you what I have seen, heard, and encountered myself: In a certain city there lived a robber who used to rob on a large scale. Once upon a time, in order to carry on his tricks, he left his own country and went into another country, leaving his wife behind him. During his absence the woman was visited by a thief: now listen to me well, and do not fall asleep. This thief came and practised such deceit on her that she took him for her husband and admitted him to her house, her true husband having been a very long time away. At last the robber returned, and, finding the thief established in his home, he was astonished, saying to himself, 'Has any kinsman of my wife's come to see her?' However, he salaamed and entered the door, when the thief exclaimed to him roughly, 'Sir, who are you?'

"'This house is mine,' answered the robber; 'my wife lives here.'

"'Nay,' said the thief, 'the woman is not your wife, but mine. You must be some bad character, and I shall send at once for the police and have you well thrashed.'

"The robber was astounded. 'Wife,' said he, 'do you not know me? I am your husband!'

"'Nonsense, man,' replied the woman, 'this is my husband—I never saw you before.'

"'This is a pretty thing!' cried the robber, and he was fain to sleep elsewhere.

"In the morning all the neighbours assembled and welcomed the robber as an old friend; and to the wife they said, 'You have made a slight mistake; this is your real husband, and the other fellow is not.' A regular fight ensued between the rival claimants, and they were carried off to the judge, when the woman settled the difficulty by saying, 'I am the wife of him who brings me home the most money.'

"Then said the thief to the robber, 'Who and what are you?'

"'I am a robber,' answered he; 'who are you?'

"'I am a thief,' said the other.

"The thief, who would by no means relinquish the woman, now said: 'Listen to me. Let us make trial of our skill. First, show me what you can do, or, if you please, I will begin. I am a thief and a cheat. If you can do more in robbery than I can perform in deceit, the woman is yours; but if otherwise, she is mine.'

"The thief then hired some fine clothing, got into a palanquin, and, going to a city, gave himself out to be a rich merchant. As he passed through the streets, he stopped at the door of a jeweller, who considered himself so honoured by a visit from one whose great fame had preceded him, that he rose up and made him a humble obeisance.

"The pretended merchant, with a lordly air, now asked, 'Have you any pearls for sale?'

"'Yes,' answered the jeweller.

"'Let me see the best you have,' said the thief.

"The jeweller immediately produced a beautiful casket, which the thief opened, and found therein several strings of pearls, which he proceeded to examine. After a pause he gave back the casket, saying, 'These are not what I require. I want pearls of a better quality than these. Have you no more?'

"The jeweller then brought out three or four other caskets, one of which the thief opened, and, while pretending to examine the worth of the contents, he adroitly cut off two strings of pearls, and, unseen by the owner, hid them in his sleeve. He then said: 'How many boxes of pearls do you possess of this description?'

"'Altogether I have seven,' answered the jeweller.

"'You shall hear from me again,' replied the thief, and, getting up, he went at once to the king, who was sitting in court, and paid his respects.

"'Well, merchant,' said the king, 'how has it fared with you since coming to my capital?'

"'O king,' answered the thief, 'I have been robbed of seven boxes of pearls of the greatest value, and, according to information which I have received, they are in the hands of a certain jeweller.'

"Immediately the king gave the thief a guard, and ordered that the jewellers' shop should be at once closed and the unfortunate man arrested.

"On their arrival at the shop, the thief pointed out the box out of which he himself had stolen the pearls, and said to the guard, 'All my caskets were like that one.' The soldiers hereupon took the box and the jeweller back to the king, to whom the thief said: 'O king, this casket is mine.' But the jeweller protested: 'Nay, your highness, this casket is not his property, but mine.'

"'If it is yours,' replied the thief, 'tell the king how many strings of pearls it contains.'

"'It contains one hundred,' at once said the jeweller.

"'No, no,' said the thief, 'not one hundred, but ninety-eight.'

"'Let the strings be counted,' commanded the king.

"This order was accordingly obeyed, when it was found, to the satisfaction of the court, that the thief had spoken truly. 'The whole of my pearl-caskets,' said the thief, 'have been stolen from me, and are now unlawfully held by this jeweller. If this casket had not been mine, how could I have known the number of strings contained in it?'

"'True,' said the king, 'the casket is evidently yours.' And he ordered the other caskets also to be delivered to him, but the jeweller was beaten with rods and cast into a prison.

"The robber, who had witnessed the whole of this knavery on the part of the thief, was amazed, and how to overreach such matchless impudence he was puzzled to say. However, he now joined him, and both the rogues went together to the woman's house and related the story.

"Now," cried the rat, "you must understand that the father of wisdom, who handed over these pearls to a common swindler and cheat, is also the father of this adorable princess. That is what I saw and what I heard, and so I have told you."

The princess was so enraged at hearing these concluding words that, being quite unable to restrain herself, she cried out to the leg of the bed: "When the morning comes you shall be cut off too, and thrown into the fire with your lying brother!"

Hardly had she spoken when the great drum was heard to resound for the second time, and all the people remarked it. "Salaam Alaikim!" cried the blacksmith's daughter, laughing. "Alaikim salaam!" answered the rat.

Some little time now passed by, when the blacksmith's daughter again broke silence.

"Delightful creature and most charming princess," said she, "you have regaled me with an excellent story. But the night is long and tedious. Pray tell me another."

The rat, who had moved his position to the third leg of the bed, answered, "Good, I will tell you what I saw with my eyes and heard with my ears. My former story was all about the thief. You shall now hear the adventure of the robber.

"It was the next day that the robber said to the thief: 'It is now my turn. It is necessary, however, that you promise not to open your mouth to say a single word, since I kept strict silence with you. Otherwise you lose the prize.'

"To this condition the thief agreed, and both started once more and travelled to the same town. For some time the robber cudgeled his brains to no purpose for some device by which to surpass the thief. 'I must contrive some scheme,' thought he, 'to have the thief imprisoned and his gains transferred to myself.' On inquiry he learnt that the king was in the habit of sleeping on the roof of his palace, which was built in a pleasant place by the river-side. Said he to the thief: 'You must of course attend me as I attended you, and be a silent witness of my work.'

"Taking some iron pegs with him, the robber went to the palace, and, by fixing the pegs in the joints of the masonry one by one, he managed to climb to the roof. When he got to the top he perceived that the king was asleep, and that he was attended by a single guard who was pacing up and down. Watching his opportunity, he cut down the guard and threw his body into the river. Then taking up the musket, he assumed the sentry's functions, and begun pacing backwards and forwards, while the thief sat down at a distance and looked on.

"After a short time the king stirred, and cried: 'Sentry!'

"'Here I am, sir,' answered the robber.

"'Come near to me,' said the king, 'and sit down, and tell me a story, that my soul may rejoice.'

"So the robber approached the monarch, and, sitting down as he was directed, he told him the story of the jeweller, the thief, and the pearls. As the story progressed the thief began to tremble with fright, and made repeated signs to the robber to change the subject, or at least not to divulge his name or to betray him; but the robber pretended not to notice him, and went on with his tale. Then suddenly breaking off, he began to tell the king his own story, and how by means of iron pegs he had scaled the palace roof and killed his sentry.

"'Good heavens!' cried the king, looking round in consternation. 'Who are you? Tell me this instant!'

"'Sire,' answered the robber, 'be not alarmed—I am the robber.'

"'And where is my sentry' asked the perplexed monarch.

"'I have just thrown his lifeless body into the river,' said the robber.

"The king was greatly alarmed. 'And yet,' thought he, 'this scoundrel might also have cut me down and disposed of me in the same way, and he didn't! He must be a good sort of fellow.' This consideration relieved the king's mind. 'Come near to me,' then said he aloud.

"'But,' replied the robber, 'I was telling your majesty the story of a thief. This person, you must know, now standing behind you, is the very thief in question, and the jeweller is innocent of any crime.' Saying these words, he led the thief forward by the ear.

"Morning now dawning, some attendants appeared, the thief was seized, and in due time the jeweller was released out of prison. Then the king, sitting on his judgment seat, gave orders that the pearls should be divided equally between the robber and the jeweller, and that the thief should be blown away from a gun. After this the robber joyfully returned home to his wife and took possession of his house.

"And now," continued the rat, "all I have to add is that the father of wisdom who rewards robbers with the property of other people is also the father of this charming lady."

Hearing these words, the princess became more angry than ever, and cried: "O lying spirit, when morning comes I will burn you too!"

Then sounded the drum for the third and last time, and the people of the city heard it, and, turning in their beds, said to their children: "To-morrow the princess will be married."

"Salaam Alaikim!" said the blacksmith's daughter.

"Alaikim salaam!" answered the rat, after which the two friends parted, the rat going his own way, while his benefactress closed her eyes and slept.

The next morning the whole city was astir, eager for news of the princess's wedding, and by common consent there was universal holiday. The blacksmith's daughter rose betimes, and, dressing herself with the utmost care, she went out to the stables, and there she saw her husband, Prince Ghool, in the costume of a groom, rubbing down a horse with curry-comb and brush. She gazed at him very tenderly for a moment, while a tear came into her eye, but she hastily recovered herself, and returned to the palace. The whole day was devoted to feastings, games, and rejoicings; and by-and-by the priest came, and in the midst of the assembled dignitaries of the court the blacksmith's daughter and the princess were united in marriage according to the forms in vogue among Mahommedans. When the ceremony was over the sham bridegroom addressed her bride and said: "I have fairly won you in spite of every difficulty, and now it is my will that for six months you are not to enter my chamber."

The wisdom of the pretended prince was so great that her father-in-law paid her the greatest possible respect and consulted her in all affairs of state, and her manners and speech were so charming that she won all hearts. One of her earliest acts of grace was to petition the king to release all the unfortunate princes who were engaged in menial attendance on her wife's horses, and to permit them to return to their homes. Her request was granted; but as she herself bore the order, she was careful while dismissing all the rest to except her own husband, and on him she laid her commands to bring to her his horse every morning saddled and bridled, and to attend her on her expeditions. Prince Ghool, noticing all his companions restored to their liberty, could scarcely on this occasions forbear crying with vexation and disappointment as he said to himself: "I alone am left in slavery!"

After many days the blacksmith's daughter went to the king, and said: "O king, a favour! Give me leave to visit my own country and my own kindred." Her prayer was granted, and she was provided with an escort of horsemen, and with every comfort for the journey both for herself and for the princess. Then she ordered Prince Ghool never to leave her horse's side, and over him she set guards lest he should attempt to escape.

After several marches had been accomplished the prince said to himself: "I perceive that we are going to my own country. Alas! what would the blacksmith's daughter say if she saw me in such a plight as this?"

When the cavalcade came within two or three marches of the capital, and had halted for the night, the blacksmith's daughter sent for her husband,

and said to him: "I have now urgent business on hand, the nature of which I cannot communicate. It is enough that I require a disguise. Do you give me your groom's clothing, and, accepting some of mine in its place, represent me in my absence. Halt here for a month. In a short time I shall see you again."

The prince, wondering at her request, obeyed, and assumed the dress of his supposed master. But she, having received his groom's clothing from a trusty attendant, together with his curry-comb and brush, locked them all up in a box, and, taking them with her, stole off in the darkness to her father's house.

A day or two having elapsed, and the blacksmith's daughter not returning, Prince Ghool said: "This prince bade me to remain here for a month with the princess and her retinue. My father is a powerful king, and his capital is near. Why should I not carry off the princess to my own home and swear that I won her?" So that night he gave order accordingly, and on the third day he arrived at his father's palace. He entered in triumph, and proclamation was made everywhere that Prince Ghool had returned, and that he had won the famous dumb princess; and when the people saw him riding through the street by the side of his father, who had gone forth with troops to escort him in, every house resounded with acclamations.

The next day Prince Ghool sent a message to the house of the blacksmith, and ordered him to send his daughter to the palace. As soon as she appeared, he said to her: "Oh, you taunted me about this princess, did you? Now what have you to say? Have I not won her?"

"Did you win her," quietly answered she, "or did I?"

"I did," protested he.

"Nay, I did," replied the girl.

She then stamped her little foot, and a servant brought in a box. When the company had been ordered to retire she unlocked the box, and took from it the old curry-comb, the brush, and the old suit of groom's clothes.

Holding them up before the prince, she asked: "Whose are these—yours or mine?"

The prince was confounded, and for a moment he could not speak. He then stammered: "They are mine!"

"Did you, then, win the princess," demanded she, "or did I?"

"You did," answered he.

"Ah," said the blacksmith's daughter, "if you with your father's ministers were not able even to tell the secret of the earthen jars, how could you possibly have won the dumb princess? But now take her, and marry her, and let us all be happy at last."

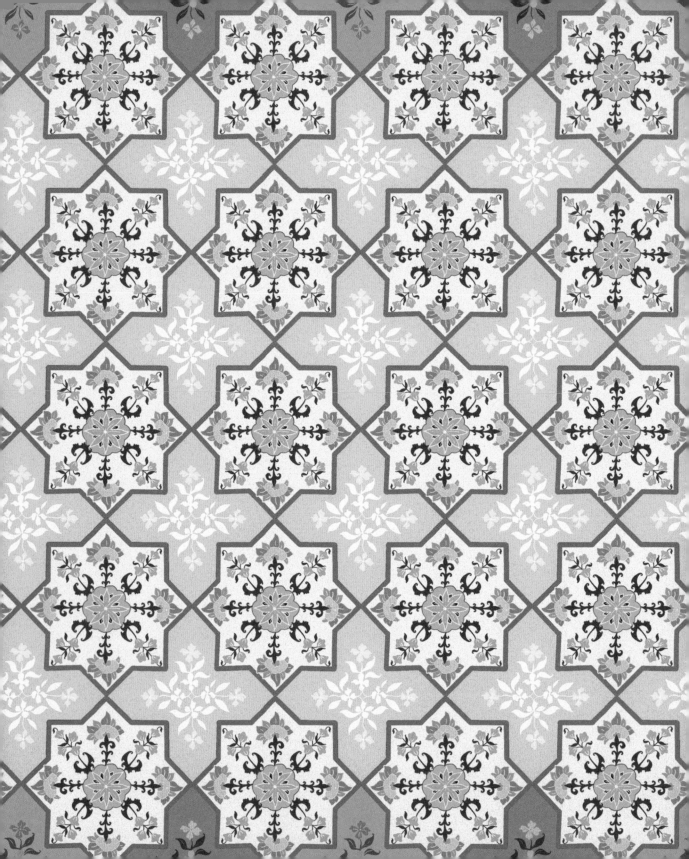

Outwitting and Outwitted

THE
GHOST-BRAHMAN

❖ ⋯❈⋯ ❖

Bengal

Once on a time there lived a poor Brahman, who not being a Kulin, found it the hardest thing in the world to get married. He went to rich people and begged of them to give him money that he might marry a wife. And a large sum of money was needed, not so much for the expenses of the wedding, as for giving to the parents of the bride. He begged from door to door, flattered many rich folk, and at last succeeded in scraping together the sum needed. The wedding took place in due time; and he brought home his wife to his mother. After a short time he said to his mother—"Mother, I have no means to support you and my wife; I must therefore go to distant countries to get money somehow or other. I may be away for years, for I won't return till I get a good sum. In the meantime I'll give you what I have; you make the best of it, and take care of my wife." The Brahman receiving his mother's blessing set out on his travels. In the evening of that very day, a ghost assuming the exact appearance of the Brahman came into the house. The newly married woman, thinking it was her husband, said to him—"How is it that you have returned so soon? You said you might be away for years; why have you changed your mind?" The ghost said—"To-day is not a lucky day, I have therefore returned home; besides, I have already got some money." The mother did not doubt but that it was her son. So the ghost lived in the house as if he was its owner, and as if he was the son of the old woman and the husband of the young woman. As the ghost and the Brahman were exactly like each other in every thing, like two peas, the people in the neighbourhood all thought that the ghost was the real Brahman. After some years the Brahman returned from his travels; and what was his surprise when he found another like him in the house. The ghost said to the Brahman—"Who are you? what business have you to come to my house?" "Who am I?" replied the Brahman, "let me ask who you are. This is my house; that is my mother, and this is my wife." The ghost said—"Why herein is a strange thing. Every one knows that this is my house, that is my wife, and yonder is my mother; and I have lived here for years. And you pretend this is your house, and that woman is your wife. Your head must have got turned, Brahman." So saying the ghost drove away the Brahman from his house. The Brahman became mute with wonder. He did not know what to do. At last he bethought himself of going to the king and of laying his case before him. The king saw the ghost-Brahman as well as the Brahman, and the one was the picture of the other; so he was in a fix, and did not know how to decide the quarrel. Day after day the Brahman went to the king and besought him to give him back his house, his wife, and his mother; and the king, not knowing what to say every time, put him off to the following day. Every day the king tells him to—"Come to-morrow;" and every day the Brahman goes away from the palace weeping and striking his forehead with the palm of his hand, and saying—"What a wicked world this is! I am driven from my own house, and another fellow has taken possession of my house and of my wife! And what a king this is! He does not do justice."

Now, it came to pass that as the Brahman went away every day from the court outside the town, he passed a spot at which a great many cow-boys used to play. They let the cows graze on the meadow, while they themselves met together under a large tree to play. And they played at royalty.

One cow-boy was elected king; another, prime minister or vizier; another, *kotwal*, or prefect of the police; and others, constables. Every day for several days together they saw the Brahman passing by weeping. One day the cow-boy king asked his vizier whether he knew why the Brahman wept every day. On the vizier not being able to answer the question, the cow-boy-king ordered one of his constables to bring the Brahman to him. One of them went and said to the Brahman—"The king requires your immediate attendance." The Brahman replied—"What for? I have just come from the king, and he put me off till to-morrow. Why does he want me again?" "It is our king that wants you—our neat-herd king," rejoined the constable. "Who is neat-herd king?" asked the Brahman. "Come and see," was the reply. The neat-herd king then asked the Brahman why he every day went away weeping. The Brahman then told him his sad story. The neat-herd king, after hearing the whole, said, "I understand your case; I will give you again all your rights. Only go to the king and ask his permission for me to decide your case." The Brahman went back to the king of the country, and begged his Majesty to send his case to the neat-herd king, who had offered to decide it. The king, whom the case had greatly puzzled, granted the permission sought. The following morning was fixed for the trial. The neat-herd king, who saw through the whole, brought with him next day a phial with a narrow neck. The Brahman and the ghost-Brahman both appeared at the bar. After a great deal of examination of witnesses and of speech-making, the neat-herd king said—"Well, I have heard enough. I'll decide the case at once. Here is this phial. Whichever of you will enter into it shall be declared by the court to be the rightful owner of the house the title of which is in dispute. Now, let me see, which of you will enter." The Brahman said—"You are a neat-herd, and your intellect is that of a neat-herd. What man can enter into such a small phial?" "If you cannot enter," said the neat-herd king, "then you are not the rightful owner. What do you say, sir, to this?" turning to the ghost-Brahman and addressing him. "If you can enter into the phial, then the house and the wife and the mother become yours." "Of course I will enter," said the ghost. And true to his word, to the wonder of all, he made himself into a small creature like an insect, and entered into the phial. The neat-herd king forthwith corked up the phial, and the ghost could not get out. Then, addressing the Brahman, the neat-herd king said, "Throw this phial into the bottom of the sea, and take possession of your house, wife, and mother." The Brahman did so, and lived happily for many years and begat sons and daughters.

Thus my story endeth,
The Natiya-thorn withereth;
"Why, O Natiya-thorn, dost wither?"
"Why does thy cow on me browse?"
"Why, O cow, dost thou browse?"
"Why does thy neat-herd not tend me?"
"Why, O neat-herd, dost not tend the cow?"
"Why does thy daughter-in-law not give me rice?"
"Why, O daughter-in-law, dost not give rice?"
"Why does my child cry?"
"Why, O child, dost thou cry?"
"Why does the ant bite me?"
"Why, O ant, dost thou bite?"
Koot! koot! koot![†]

[†]   According to the author of this story, orthodox Bengali storytellers used to repeat these lines at the end of every tale.

BOPOLÛCHÎ

> ❖ ┄┄•❀•┄┄ ❖

Punjab

O nce upon a time a number of young girls went to draw water at the village well, and whilst they were filling their jars, fell a-talking of their betrothals and weddings.

Said one—"My uncle will soon be coming with the bridal presents, and he is to bring the finest clothes imaginable."

Said a second—"And my uncle-in-law is coming, I know, bringing the most delicious sweetmeats you could think of."

Said a third—"Oh, my uncle will be here in no time, with the rarest jewels in the world."

But Bopolûchî, the prettiest girl of them all, looked sad, for she was an orphan, and had no one to arrange a marriage for her. Nevertheless she was too proud to remain silent, so she said gaily—"And my uncle is coming also, bringing me fine dresses, fine food, and fine jewels."

Now a wandering pedlar, who sold sweet scents and cosmetics of all sorts to the country women, happened to be sitting near the well, and heard what Bopolûchî said. Being much struck by her beauty and spirit, he determined to marry her himself, and the very next day, disguised as a well-to-do farmer, he came to Bopolûchî's house laden with trays upon trays full of fine dresses, fine food, and fine jewels; for he was not a real pedlar, but a wicked robber, ever so rich.

Bopolûchî could hardly believe her eyes, for everything was just as she had foretold, and the robber said he was her father's brother, who had been away in the world for years, and had now come back to arrange her marriage with one of his sons, her cousin.

Hearing this, Bopolûchî of course believed it all, and was ever so much pleased; so she packed up the few things she possessed in a bundle, and set off with the robber in high spirits.

But as they went along the road, a crow sitting on a branch croaked—

"Bopolûchî, 'tis a pity!

You have lost your wits, my pretty!

'Tis no uncle that relieves you,

But a robber who deceives you!"

"Uncle!" said Bopolûchî, "that crow croaks funnily. What does it say?"

"Pooh!" returned the robber, "all the crows in this country croak like that."

A little further on they met a peacock, which, as soon as it caught sight of the pretty little maiden, began to scream—

"Bopolûchî, 'tis a pity!

You have lost your wits, my pretty!

'Tis no uncle that relieves you,

But a robber who deceives you!"

"Uncle!" said the girl, "that peacock screams funnily. What does it say?"

"Pooh!" returned the robber, "all peacocks scream like that in this country."

By and by a jackal slunk across the road; the moment it saw poor pretty Bopolûchî it began to howl—

"Bopolûchî, 'tis a pity!

You have lost your wits, my pretty!

'Tis no uncle that relieves you,

But a robber who deceives you!"

"Uncle!" said the maiden, "that jackal howls funnily. What does it say?"

"Pooh!" returned the robber, "all jackals howl like that in this country."

So poor pretty Bopolûchî journeyed on till they reached the robber's house. Then he told her who he was, and how he intended to marry her himself. She wept and cried bitterly, but the robber had no pity, and left her in charge of his old, oh! ever so old mother, while he went out to make arrangements for the marriage feast.

Now Bopolûchî had such beautiful hair that it reached right down to her ankles, but the old mother hadn't a hair on her old bald head.

"Daughter!" said the old, ever so old mother, as she was putting the bridal dress on Bopolûchî, "how ever did you manage to get such beautiful hair?"

"Well," replied Bopolûchî, "my mother made it grow by pounding my head in the big mortar for husking rice. At every stroke of the pestle my hair grew longer and longer. I assure you it is a plan that never fails."

"Perhaps it would make *my* hair grow!" said the old woman eagerly.

"Perhaps it would!" quoth cunning Bopolûchî.

So the old, ever so old mother put her head in the mortar, and Bopolûchî pounded away with such a will that the old lady died.

Then Bopolûchî dressed the dead body in the scarlet bridal dress, seated it on the low bridal chair, drew the veil well over the face, and put the spinning-wheel in front of it, so that when the robber came home he might think it was the bride. Then she put on the old mother's clothes, and seizing her own bundle, stepped out of the house as quickly as possible.

On her way home she met the robber, who was returning with a stolen millstone, to grind the corn for the wedding feast, on his head. She was dreadfully frightened, and slipped behind the hedge, so as not to be seen. But the robber, not recognising her in the old mother's dress, thought she was some strange woman from a neighbouring village, and so to avoid being seen he slipped behind the other hedge. Thus Bopolûchî reached home in safety.

Meanwhile, the robber, having come to his house, saw the figure in bridal scarlet sitting on the bridal chair, spinning, and of course thought it was Bopolûchî. So he called to her to help him down with the mill-stone, but she didn't answer. He called again, but still she didn't answer. Then he fell into a rage, and threw the millstone at her head. The figure toppled over, and lo and behold! it was not Bopolûchî at all, but his old, ever so old mother! Whereupon the robber wept, and beat his breast, thinking he had killed her; but when he discovered pretty Bopolûchî had run away, he became wild with rage, and determined to bring her back somehow.

Now Bopolûchî was convinced that the robber would try to carry her off, so every night she begged a new lodging in some friend's house, leaving her own little bed in her own little house quite empty; but after a month or so she had come to the end of her friends, and did not like to ask any of them to give her shelter a second time. So she determined to brave it out and sleep at home, whatever happened; but she took a bill-hook to bed with her. Sure enough, in the very middle of the night four men crept in, and each seizing a leg of the bed, lifted it up and walked off, the robber himself having hold of the leg close behind her head. Bopolûchî was wide awake, but pretended to be fast asleep, until she came to a wild deserted spot, where the thieves were off their guard; then she whipped out the bill-hook, and in a twinkling cut off the heads of the two thieves at the foot of the bed. Turning round quickly, she did the same to the other thief at the head, but the robber himself ran away in a terrible fright, and scrambled like a wild cat up a tree close by before she could reach him.

"Come down!" cried brave Bopolûchî, brandishing the bill-hook, "and fight it out!"

But the robber would not come down; so Bopolûchî gathered all the sticks she could find, piled them round the tree, and set fire to them. Of course the tree caught fire also, and the robber, half stifled with the smoke, tried to jump down, and was killed.

After that, Bopolûchî went to the robber's house and carried off all the gold and silver, jewels and clothes, that were hidden there, coming back to the village so rich that she could marry any one she pleased. And that was the end of Bopolûchî's adventures.

THE SON of
SEVEN MOTHERS

Punjab

Once upon a time there lived a King who had seven wives, but no children. This was a great grief to him, especially when he remembered that on his death there would be no heir to inherit the kingdom.

Now, one day, a poor old *fakir*, or religious devotee, came to the King and said, "Your prayers are heard, your desire shall be accomplished, and each of your seven queens shall bear a son."

The King's delight at this promise knew no bounds, and he gave orders for appropriate festivities to be prepared against the coming event throughout the length and breadth of the land.

Meanwhile the seven Queens lived luxuriously in a splendid palace, attended by hundreds of female slaves, and fed to their hearts' content on sweetmeats and confectionery.

Now the King was very fond of hunting, and one day, before he started, the seven Queens sent him a message saying, "May it please our dearest lord not to hunt towards the north to-day, for we have dreamt bad dreams, and fear lest evil should befall you."

The King, to allay their anxiety, promised regard for their wishes, and set out towards the south; but as luck would have it, although he hunted diligently, he found no game. Nor had he greater success to the east or west, so that, being a keen sportsman, and determined not to go home empty-handed, he forgot all about his promise, and turned to the north. Here also he met at first with no reward, but just as he had made up his mind to give up for that day, a white hind with golden horns and silver hoofs flashed past him into a thicket. So quickly did it pass, that he scarcely saw it; nevertheless a burning desire to capture and possess the beautiful strange creature filled his breast. He instantly ordered his attendants to form a ring round the thicket, and so encircle the hind; then, gradually narrowing the circle, he pressed forward till he could distinctly see the white hind panting in the midst. Nearer and nearer he advanced, when, just as he thought to lay hold of the beautiful strange creature, it gave one mighty bound, leapt clean over the King's head, and fled towards the mountains. Forgetful of all else, the King, setting spurs to his horse, followed at full speed. On, on he galloped, leaving his retinue far behind, but keeping the white hind in view, and never drawing bridle, until, finding himself in a narrow ravine with no outlet, he reined in his steed. Before him stood a miserable hovel, into which, being tired after his long unsuccessful chase, he entered to ask for a drink of water. An old woman, seated in the hut at a spinning-wheel, answered his request by calling to her daughter, and immediately from an inner room came a maiden so lovely and charming, so white-skinned and golden-haired, that the King was transfixed by astonishment at seeing so beautiful a sight in the wretched hovel.

She held the vessel of water to the King's lips, and as he drank he looked into her eyes, and then it became clear to him that the girl was no other than the white hind with the golden horns and silver feet he had chased so far.

Her beauty bewitched him completely, and he fell on his knees, begging her to return with him as his bride; but she only laughed, saying seven Queens were quite enough even for a King to manage. However, when he would take no refusal, but implored her to have pity on him, and promised her everything she could desire, she replied, "Give me the eyes of your seven wives, and then perhaps I may believe that you mean what you say."

The King was so carried away by the glamour of the white hind's magical beauty, that he went home at once, had the eyes of his seven Queens taken out, and, after throwing the poor blind creatures into a noisome dungeon whence they could not escape, set off once more for the hovel in the ravine, bearing with him his loathsome offering. But the white hind only laughed cruelly when she saw the fourteen eyes, and threading them as a necklace, flung it round her mother's neck, saying, "Wear that, little mother, as a keepsake, whilst I am away in the King's palace."

Then she went back with the bewitched monarch as his bride, and he gave her the seven Queens' rich clothes and jewels to wear, the seven Queens' palace to live in, and the seven Queens' slaves to wait upon her; so that she really had everything even a witch could desire.

Now, very soon after the seven wretched, hapless Queens were cast into prison, the first Queen's baby was born. It was a handsome boy, but the Queens were so desperately hungry that they killed the child at once, and, dividing it into seven portions, ate it. All except the youngest Queen, who saved her portion secretly.

The next day the second Queen's baby was born, and they did the same with it, and with all the babies in turn, one after the other, until the seventh and youngest Queen's baby was born on the seventh day. But when the other six Queens came to the young mother, and wanted to take it away, saying, "Give us your child to eat, as you have eaten ours!" she produced the six pieces of the other babies untouched, and answered, "Not so! here are six pieces for you; eat them, and leave my child alone. You cannot complain, for you have each your fair share, neither more nor less."

Now, though the other Queens were very jealous that the youngest amongst them should by forethought and self-denial have saved her baby's life, they could say nothing; for, as the young mother had told them, they received their full share. And though at first they disliked the handsome little boy, he soon proved so useful to them, that ere long they all looked on him as their son. Almost as soon as he was born he began scraping at the mud wall of their dungeon, and in an incredibly short space of time had made a hole big enough for him to crawl through. Through this he disappeared, returning in an hour or so laden with sweetmeats, which he divided equally amongst the seven blind Queens.

As he grew older he enlarged the hole, and slipped out two or three times every day to play with the little nobles in the town. No one knew who the tiny boy was, but everybody liked him, and he was so full of funny tricks and antics, so merry and bright, that he was sure to be rewarded by some girdle-cakes, a handful of parched grain, or some sweetmeats. All these things he brought home to his seven mothers, as he loved to call the seven blind Queens, who by his help lived on in their dungeon when all the world thought they had starved to death ages before.

At last, when he was quite a big lad, he one day took his bow and arrow, and went out to seek for game. Coming by chance upon the palace where the white hind lived in wicked splendour and magnificence, he saw some pigeons fluttering round the white marble turrets, and, taking good aim, shot one dead. It came tumbling past the very window where the white Queen was sitting; she rose to see what was the matter, and looked out. At the first glance at the handsome young lad standing there bow in hand, she knew by witchcraft that it was the King's son.

She nearly died of envy and spite, determining to destroy the lad without delay; therefore, sending a servant to bring him to her presence, she asked him if he would sell her the pigeon he had just shot.

"No," replied the sturdy lad, "the pigeon is for my seven blind mothers, who live in the noisome dungeon, and who would die if I did not bring them food."

"Poor souls!" cried the cunning white witch; "would you not like to bring them their eyes again? Give me the pigeon, my dear, and I faithfully promise to show you where to find them."

Hearing this, the lad was delighted beyond measure, and gave up the pigeon at once. Whereupon the white Queen told him to seek her mother without delay, and ask for the eyes which she wore as a necklace.

"She will not fail to give them," said the cruel Queen, "if you show her this token on which I have written what I want done."

So saying, she gave the lad a piece of broken potsherd, with these words inscribed on it—"Kill the bearer at once, and sprinkle his blood like water!"

Now, as the son of seven mothers could not read, he took the fatal message cheerfully, and set off to find the white Queen's mother.

But while he was journeying he passed through a town, where every one of the inhabitants looked so sad that he could not help asking what was the matter. They told him it was because the King's only daughter refused to marry; so when her father died there would be no heir to the throne. They greatly feared she must be out of her mind, for though every good-looking young man in the kingdom had been shown to her, she declared she would only marry one who was the son of seven mothers, and of course no one had ever heard of such a thing. Still the King, in despair, had ordered every man who entered the city gates to be led before the Princess in case she might relent. So, much to the lad's impatience, for he was in an immense hurry to find his mothers' eyes, he was dragged into the presence-chamber.

No sooner did the Princess catch sight of him than she blushed, and, turning to the King, said, "Dear father, this is my choice!"

Never were such rejoicings as these few words produced. The inhabitants nearly went wild with joy, but the son of seven mothers said he would not marry the Princess unless they first let him recover his mothers' eyes. Now when the beautiful bride heard his story, she asked to see the potsherd, for she was very learned and clever; so much so that on seeing the treacherous words, she said nothing, but taking another similarly-shaped bit of potsherd, wrote on it these words—"Take care of this lad, give him all he desires," and returned it to the son of seven mothers, who, none the wiser, set off on his quest.

Ere long, he arrived at the hovel in the ravine, where the white witch's mother, a hideous old creature, grumbled dreadfully on reading the message, especially when the lad asked for the necklace of eyes. Nevertheless she took it off, and gave it him, saying, "There are only thirteen of 'em now, for I ate one last week, when I was hungry."

The lad, however, was only too glad to get any at all, so he hurried home as fast as he could to his seven mothers, and gave two eyes apiece to the six elder Queens; but to the youngest he gave one, saying, "Dearest little mother!—I will be your other eye always!"

After this he set off to marry the Princess, as he had promised, but when passing by the white Queen's palace he again saw some pigeons on the roof. Drawing his bow, he shot one, and again it came fluttering past the window. Then the white hind looked out, and lo! there was the King's son alive and well.

She cried with hatred and disgust, but sending for the lad, asked him how he had returned so soon, and when she heard how he had brought home the thirteen eyes, and given them to the seven blind Queens, she could hardly restrain her rage. Nevertheless she pretended to be charmed with his success, and told him that if he would give her this pigeon also, she would reward him with the Jôgi's wonderful cow, whose milk flows all day long, and makes a pond as big as a kingdom. The lad, nothing loath, gave her the pigeon; whereupon, as before, she bade him go ask her mother for the cow, and gave him a potsherd whereon was written—"Kill this lad without fail, and sprinkle his blood like water!"

But on the way, the son of seven mothers looked in on the Princess, just to tell her how he came to be delayed, and she, after reading the message on the potsherd, gave him another in its stead; so that when the lad reached the old hag's hut and asked her for the Jôgi's cow, she could not refuse, but told the boy how to find it; and, bidding him of all things not to be afraid of the eighteen thousand demons who kept watch and ward over the treasure, told him to be off before she became too angry at her daughter's foolishness in thus giving away so many good things.

Then the lad did as he had been told bravely. He journeyed on and on till he came to a milk-white pond, guarded by the eighteen thousand demons. They were really frightful to behold, but, plucking up courage, he whistled a tune as he walked through them, looking neither to the right nor the left. By and by he came upon the Jôgi's cow, tall, white, and beautiful, while the Jôgi himself, who was king of all the demons, sat milking her day and night, and the milk streamed from her udder, filling the milk-white tank.

The Jôgi, seeing the lad, called out fiercely, "What do you want here?"

Then the lad answered, according to the old hag's bidding, "I want your skin, for King Indra is making a new kettledrum, and says your skin is nice and tough."

Upon this the Jôgi began to shiver and shake (for no Jinn or Jôgi dares disobey King Indra's command), and, falling at the lad's feet, cried, "If you will spare me I will give you anything I possess, even my beautiful white cow!"

To this, the son of seven mothers, after a little pretended hesitation, agreed, saying that after all it would not be difficult to find a nice tough skin like the Jôgi's elsewhere; so, driving the wonderful cow before him, he set off homewards. The seven Queens were delighted to possess so marvellous an animal, and though they toiled from morning till night making curds and whey, besides selling milk to the confectioners, they could not use half the cow gave, and became richer and richer day by day.

Seeing them so comfortably off, the son of seven mothers started with a light heart to marry the Princess; but when passing the white hind's palace he could not resist sending a bolt at some pigeons which were cooing on the parapet, and for the third time one fell dead just beneath the window where the white Queen was sitting. Looking out, she saw the lad hale and hearty standing before her, and grew whiter than ever with rage and spite.

She sent for him to ask how he had returned so soon, and when she heard how kindly her mother had received him, she very nearly had a fit; however, she dissembled her feelings as well as she could, and, smiling sweetly, said she was glad to have been able to fulfil her promise, and that if he would give her this third pigeon, she would do yet more for him than she had done before, by giving him the million-fold rice, which ripens in one night.

The lad was of course delighted at the very idea, and, giving up the pigeon, set off on his quest, armed as before with a potsherd, on which was written, "Do not fail this time. Kill the lad, and sprinkle his blood like water!"

But when he looked in on his Princess, just to prevent her becoming anxious about him, she asked to see the potsherd as usual, and substituted another, on which was written, "Yet again give this lad all he requires, for his blood shall be as your blood!"

Now when the old hag saw this, and heard how the lad wanted the million-fold rice which ripens in a single night, she fell into the most furious rage, but being terribly afraid of her daughter, she controlled herself, and bade the boy go and find the field guarded by eighteen millions of demons, warning him on no account to look back after having plucked the tallest spike of rice, which grew in the centre.

So the son of seven mothers set off, and soon came to the field where, guarded by eighteen millions of demons, the million-fold rice grew. He walked on bravely, looking neither to the right nor left, till he reached the centre and plucked the tallest ear; but as he turned homewards a thousand sweet voices rose behind him, crying in tenderest accents, "Pluck me too! oh, please pluck me too!" He looked back, and lo! there was nothing left of him but a little heap of ashes!

Now as time passed by and the lad did not return, the old hag grew uneasy, remembering the message "his blood shall be as your blood"; so she set off to see what had happened.

Soon she came to the heap of ashes, and knowing by her arts what it was, she took a little water, and kneading the ashes into a paste, formed it into the likeness of a man; then, putting a drop of blood from her little finger into its mouth, she blew on it, and instantly the son of seven mothers started up as well as ever.

"Don't you disobey orders again!" grumbled the old hag, "or next time I'll leave you alone. Now be off, before I repent of my kindness!"

So the son of seven mothers returned joyfully to the seven Queens, who, by the aid of the million-fold rice, soon became the richest people in the kingdom. Then they celebrated their son's marriage to the clever Princess with all imaginable pomp; but the bride was so clever, she would not rest until she had made known her husband to his father, and punished the wicked white witch. So she made her husband build a palace exactly like the one in which the seven Queens had lived, and in which the white witch now dwelt in splendour. Then, when all was prepared, she bade her husband give a grand feast to the King. Now the King had heard much of the mysterious son of seven mothers, and his marvellous wealth, so he gladly accepted the invitation; but what was his astonishment when on entering the palace he found it was a facsimile of his own in every particular! And when his host, richly attired, led him straight to the private hall, where on royal thrones sat the seven Queens, dressed as he had last seen them, he was speechless with surprise, until the Princess, coming forward, threw herself at his feet, and told him the whole story. Then the King awoke from his enchantment, and his anger rose against the wicked white hind who had bewitched him so long, until he could not contain himself. So she was put to death, and her grave ploughed over, and after that the seven Queens returned to their own splendid palace, and everybody lived happily.

THE
INDIGENT BRAHMAN

Bengal

There was a Brahman who had a wife and four children. He was very poor. With no resources in the world, he lived chiefly on the benefactions of the rich. His gains were considerable when marriages were celebrated or funeral ceremonies were performed; but as his parishioners did not marry every day, neither did they die every day, he found it difficult to make the two ends meet. His wife often rebuked him for his inability to give her adequate support, and his children often went about naked and hungry. But though poor he was a good man. He was diligent in his devotions; and there was not a single day in his life in which he did not say his prayers at stated hours. His tutelary deity was the goddess Durga, the consort of Siva, the creative Energy of the Universe. On no day did he either drink water or taste food till he had written in red ink the name of Durga at least one hundred and eight times; while throughout the day he incessantly uttered the ejaculation, "O Durga! O Durga! have mercy upon me." Whenever he felt anxious on account of his poverty and his inability to support his wife and children, he groaned out—"Durga! Durga! Durga!"

One day, being very sad, he went to a forest many miles distant from the village in which he lived, and indulging his grief wept bitter tears. He prayed in the following manner:—"O Durga! O Mother Bhagavati!

wilt thou not make an end of my misery? Were I alone in the world, I should not have been sad on account of poverty; but thou hast given me a wife and children. Give me, O Mother, the means to support them." It so happened that on that day and on that very spot the god Siva and his wife Durga were taking their morning walk. The goddess Durga, on seeing the Brahman at a distance, said to her divine husband—"O Lord of Kailas! do you see that Brahman? He is always taking my name on his lips and offering the prayer that I should deliver him out of his troubles. Can we not, my lord, do something for the poor Brahman, oppressed as he is with the cares of a growing family? We should give him enough to make him comfortable. As the poor man and his family have never enough to eat, I propose that you give him a *handi* [1] which should yield him an inexhaustible supply of *mudki*." [2] The lord of Kailas readily agreed to the proposal of his divine consort, and by his decree created on the spot a *handi* possessing the required quality. Durga then, calling the Brahman to her, said,—"O Brahman! I have often thought of your pitiable case. Your repeated prayers have at last moved my compassion. Here is a *handi* for you. When you turn it upside down and shake it, it will pour down a never-ceasing shower of the finest *mudki*, which will not end till you restore the *handi* to its proper position. Yourself, your wife, and your children can eat as much *mudki* as you like, and you can also sell as much as you like." The Brahman, delighted beyond measure at obtaining so inestimable a treasure, made obeisance to the goddess, and, taking the *handi* in his hand, proceeded towards his house as fast as his legs could carry him. But he had not gone many yards when he thought of testing the efficacy of the wonderful vessel. Accordingly he turned the *handi* upside down and shook it, when, lo, and behold! a quantity of the finest *mudki* he had ever seen fell to the ground.

---

1. *Handi* is an earthen pot, generally used in cooking food.
2. *Mudki*, fried paddy boiled dry in treacle or sugar.

He tied the sweetmeat in his sheet and walked on. It was now noon, and the Brahman was hungry; but he could not eat without his ablutions and his prayers. As he saw in the way an inn, and not far from it a tank, he purposed to halt there that he might bathe, say his prayers, and then eat the much-desired *mudki*. The Brahman sat at the innkeeper's shop, put the *handi* near him, smoked tobacco, besmeared his body with mustard oil, and before proceeding to bathe in the adjacent tank gave the *handi* in charge to the innkeeper, begging him again and again to take especial care of it.

When the Brahman went to his bath and his devotions, the innkeeper thought it strange that he should be so careful as to the safety of his earthen vessel. There must be something valuable in the *handi*, he thought, otherwise why should the Brahman take so much thought about it? His curiosity being excited he opened the *handi*, and to his surprise found that it contained nothing. What can be the meaning of this? thought the innkeeper within himself. Why should the Brahman care so much for an empty *handi*? He took up the vessel, and began to examine it carefully; and when, in the course of examination, he turned the *handi* upside down, a quantity of the finest *mudki* fell from it, and went on falling without intermission. The innkeeper called his wife and children to witness this unexpected stroke of good fortune. The showers of the sugared fried paddy were so copious that they filled all the vessels and jars of the innkeeper. He resolved to appropriate to himself this precious *handi*, and accordingly put in its place another *handi* of the same size and make. The ablutions and devotions of the Brahman being now over, he came to the shop in wet clothes reciting holy texts of the Vedas. Putting on dry clothes, he wrote on a sheet of paper the name of Durga one hundred and eight times in red ink; after which he broke his fast on the *mudki* his *handi* had already given him. Thus refreshed, and being about to resume his journey homewards, he called for his *handi*, which the innkeeper delivered to him, adding—"There, sir, is your *handi*; it is just where you put it; no one has touched it." The Brahman, without suspecting anything, took up the *handi* and proceeded on his journey; and as he walked on, he congratulated himself on his singular good fortune. "How agreeably," he thought within himself, "will my poor wife be surprised! How greedily the children will devour the *mudki* of heaven's own manufacture! I shall soon become rich, and lift up my head with the best of them all." The pains of travelling were considerably alleviated by these joyful anticipations. He reached his house, and calling his wife and children, said—"Look now at what I have brought. This *handi* that you see is an unfailing source of wealth and contentment. You will see what a stream of the finest *mudki* will flow from it when I turn it upside down." The Brahman's good wife, hearing of *mudki* falling from the *handi* unceasingly, thought that her husband must have gone mad; and she was confirmed in her opinion when she found that nothing fell from the vessel though it was turned upside down again and again. Overwhelmed with grief, the Brahman concluded that the innkeeper must have played a trick with him; he must have stolen the *handi* Durga had given him, and put a common one in its stead. He went back the next day to the innkeeper, and charged him with having changed his *handi*. The innkeeper put on a fit of anger, expressed surprise at the Brahman's impudence in charging him with theft, and drove him away from his shop.

The Brahman then bethought himself of an interview with the goddess Durga who had given him the *handi*, and accordingly went to the forest where he had met her. Siva and Durga again favoured the Brahman with an interview. Durga said—"So, you have lost the *handi* I gave you. Here is another, take it and make good use of it." The Brahman, elated with joy, made obeisance to the divine couple, took up the vessel, and went on his way. He had not gone far when he turned it upside down, and shook it in order to see whether any *mudki* would fall from it. Horror of horrors! instead of sweetmeats about a score of demons, of gigantic size and grim visage, jumped out of the *handi*, and began to belabour the astonished

Brahman with blows, fisticuffs and kicks. He had the presence of mind to turn up the *handi* and to cover it, when the demons forthwith disappeared. He concluded that this new *handi* had been given him only for the punishment of the innkeeper. He accordingly went to the innkeeper, gave him the new *handi* in charge, begged of him carefully to keep it till he returned from his ablutions and prayers. The innkeeper, delighted with this second godsend, called his wife and children, and said—"This is another *handi* brought here by the same Brahman who brought the *handi* of *mudki*. This time, I hope, it is not *mudki* but *sandesa*.[3] Come, be ready with baskets and vessels, and I'll turn the *handi* upside down and shake it." This was no sooner done than scores of fierce demons started up, who caught hold of the innkeeper and his family and belaboured them mercilessly. They also began upsetting the shop, and would have completely destroyed it, if the victims had not besought the Brahman, who had by this time returned from his ablutions, to show mercy to them and send away the terrible demons. The Brahman acceded to the innkeeper's request, he dismissed the demons by shutting up the vessel; he got the former *handi*, and with the two *handis* went to his native village.

On reaching home the Brahman shut the door of his house, turned the *mudki-handi* upside down, and shook it; the result was an unceasing stream of the finest *mudki* that any confectioner in the country could produce. The man, his wife, and their children devoured the sweetmeat to their hearts' content; all the available earthen pots and pans of the house were filled with it; and the Brahman resolved the next day to turn confectioner, to open a shop in his house, and sell *mudki*. On the very day the shop was opened, the whole village came to the Brahman's house to buy the wonderful *mudki*. They had never seen such *mudki* in their life, it was so sweet, so white, so large, so luscious; no confectioner in the village or any town

---

3. A sort of sweetmeat made of curds and sugar.

in the country had ever manufactured anything like it. The reputation of the Brahman's *mudki* extended, in a few days, beyond the bounds of the village, and people came from remote parts to purchase it. Cartloads of the sweetmeat were sold every day, and the Brahman in a short time became very rich. He built a large brick house, and lived like a nobleman of the land. Once, however, his property was about to go to wreck and ruin. His children one day by mistake shook the wrong *handi*, when a large number of demons dropped down and caught hold of the Brahman's wife and children and were striking them mercilessly, when happily the Brahman came into the house and turned up the *handi*. In order to prevent a similar catastrophe in future, the Brahman shut up the demon-*handi* in a private room to which his children had no access.

Pure and uninterrupted prosperity, however, is not the lot of mortals; and though the demon-*handi* was put aside, what security was there that an accident might not befall the *mudki-handi*? One day, during the absence of the Brahman and his wife from the house, the children decided upon shaking the *handi*; but as each of them wished to enjoy the pleasure of shaking it there was a general struggle to get it, and in the *mêlée* the *handi* fell to the ground and broke. It is needless to say that the Brahman, when on reaching home he heard of the disaster, became inexpressibly sad. The children were of course well cudgelled, but no flogging of children could replace the magical *handi*. After some days he again went to the forest, and offered many a prayer for Durga's favour. At last Siva and Durga again appeared to him, and heard how the *handi* had been broken. Durga gave him another *handi*, accompanied with the following caution—"Brahman, take care of this *handi*; if you again break it or lose it, I'll not give you another." The Brahman made obeisance, and went away to his house at one stretch without halting anywhere. On reaching home he shut the door of his house, called his wife to him, turned the *handi* upside down, and began to shake it. They were only expecting *mudki* to drop from it, but instead of *mudki* a perennial stream of beautiful *sandesa* issued from it. And such *sandesa*! No confectioner of Burra Bazar ever made its like. It was more the food of gods than of men. The Brahman forthwith set up a shop for selling *sandesa*, the fame of which soon drew crowds of customers from all parts of the country. At all festivals, at all marriage feasts, at all funeral celebrations, at all *Pujas*, no one bought any other *sandesa* than the Brahman's. Every day, and every hour, many jars of gigantic size, filled with the delicious sweetmeat, were sent to all parts of the country.

The wealth of the Brahman excited the envy of the Zemindar of the village, who, having heard that the *sandesa* was not manufactured but dropped from a *handi*, devised a plan for getting possession of the miraculous vessel. At the celebration of his son's marriage he held a great feast, to which were invited hundreds of people. As many mountain-loads of *sandesa* would be required for the purpose, the Zemindar proposed that the Brahman should bring the magical *handi* to the house in which the feast was held. The Brahman at first refused to take it there; but as the Zemindar insisted on its being carried to his own house, he reluctantly consented to take it there. After many Himalayas of *sandesa* had been shaken out, the *handi* was taken possession of by the Zemindar, and the Brahman was insulted and driven out of the house. The Brahman, without giving vent to anger in the least, quietly went to his house, and taking the demon-*handi* in his hand, came back to the door of the Zemindar's house. He turned the *handi* upside down and shook it, on which a hundred demons started up as from the vasty deep and enacted a scene which it is impossible to describe. The hundreds of guests that had been bidden to the feast were caught hold of by the unearthly visitants and beaten; the women were dragged by their hair from the Zenana and dashed about amongst the men; while the big and burly Zemindar was driven about from room to room like a bale of cotton. If the demons had been allowed to do their will only for a few minutes longer, all the men would have been killed, and the very house razed to the ground.

The Zemindar fell prostrate at the feet of the Brahman and begged for mercy. Mercy was shown him, and the demons were removed. After that the Brahman was no more disturbed by the Zemindar or by any one else; and he lived many years in great happiness and enjoyment.

Thus my story endeth,

The natiya-thorn withereth;

"Why, O natiya-thorn, dost wither?"

"Why does thy cow on me browse?"

"Why, O cow, dost thou browse?"

"Why does thy neat-herd not tend me?"

"Why, O neat-herd, dost not tend the cow?"

"Why does thy daughter-in-law not give me rice?"

"Why, O daughter-in-law, dost not give rice?"

"Why does my child cry?"

"Why, O child, dost thou cry?"

"Why does the ant bite me?"

"Why, O ant, dost thou bite?"

Koot! koot! koot!

THE KING
and the ROBBERS

❖ ⋯•❖•⋯ ❖

Punjab

In former days it was the delight of kings and princes to disguise themselves and to visit the streets of their cities, both to seek adventures and to learn the habits and opinions of their subjects. One night the famous Sultan Mahmoud of Ghuzni dressed himself up, and, assuming the character of a thief, went into the streets. He there fell in with a gang of notorious robbers, and, joining himself to their company, he gave himself out as a desperate villain, saying:

"If you are thieves, I am a thief too; so let us go and try our good fortune together."

They all agreed. "Be it so," said they; "but before we set out let us compare notes, and see who possesses the strongest point for the business in hand, and let him be our captain."

"My strongest point," said one, "is my hearing. I can distinguish and understand the speech of dogs and of wolves."

"Mine," said the next, "is my hands, with which I am so practised that I can jerk a rope to the tops of the highest houses."

"And mine," said another, "is my strength of arm. I can force my way through any wall, however stoutly built."

"My chief point," said the fourth, "is my sense of smell. Show me a house, and I will reveal to you whether it is rich or poor, whether it is full or empty."

"And mine," said the fifth robber, "is my keenness of eyesight. If I meet a man on the darkest night I can detect him and point him out in the daytime."

The king now spoke and said: "My strong point is my beard. I have only to wag my beard, and a man sentenced to be hanged is released immediately."

"Then you shall be our captain!" cried all the robbers at once, "since hanging is the only thing of which we are afraid."

So the king was unanimously chosen as leader, and away the six confederates started. The house which they agreed to rob that night was the king's palace. When they arrived under the walls a dog suddenly sprang out and began to bark.

"What is he saying?" asked one.

"The dog is saying," said the robber with the fine ear, "that the king himself is one of our company."

"Then the dog lies," answered the other, "for that cannot be."

The robber who was so dexterous with his hands now threw up a rope-ladder, which attached itself to a lofty balcony, and enabled the party to mount to the top of one of the houses.

"Do you smell any money here?" said one to the robber whose scent was his principal boast.

The man went smelling about all over the roof, and at last said: "This must be some poor widow's quarters, for there is neither gold nor silver in the place. Let us go on."

The robbers now crept cautiously along the flat tops of the houses until they came to a towering wall, richly carved and painted, and the robber of the keen scent began smelling again. "Ah!" exclaimed he, "here we are! This is the king's treasure-house. Ho, Strong-arm, do you break open a way through!"

The robber of the strong arm now proceeded to dislodge the wood-work and the stones, until at last he had pierced the wall, and effected an entrance into the house. The rest of the gang speedily followed, and their search was rewarded by the coffers full of gold which they found there, and which they passed out through the aperture, and carried away. Well laden, they all by common consent hastened to one of their favourite haunts, where the spoil was divided, the king also receiving his share with the rest, while at the same time he informed himself of the robbers' names and learnt their places of abode. After this, as the night was far advanced, they separated, and the king returned alone to his palace.

The next morning the robbery was discovered and the city cried by the officers of justice. But the king, without a word, went into his audience-chamber, where he took his seat as usual. He then addressed his minister, and told him to send and arrest the robbers. "Go to such and such a street," said he, "in the lower quarter of the city, and there you will find the house. Here are the names of the criminals. Let them be taken before the judge and sentenced, and then produce them here."

The minister at once left the presence, and taking with him some attendants, he proceeded with all dispatch to the street in question, found and arrested the robbers, and took them before the judge. As the evidence of their guilt was conclusive, they made a full confession and implored mercy, but the judge condemned them all to be hanged, and sent them before the king. As soon as they appeared the king looked sternly at them, and demanded what they had to allege in extenuation that their sentence should not be carried out. Then they all began to make excuses, excepting the one whose special gift it was to recognise in the day those whom he had met at night. He, looking fixedly at the king, cried out, to the surprise of his comrades: "The moment has arrived for the wagging of the beard."

The king, hearing his words, gravely wagged his beard as a signal that the executioners should retire, and having enjoyed a hearty laugh with his chance acquaintances of the preceding night, he feasted them well, gave them some good advice, and restored them to their liberty.

"The moral of this story," continued the story-teller, "is this: The whole world is in darkness. At the last day no faculty, however strong, will avail a man but that which will enable him to discern God Himself."

THE
BRAHMARÂKSHASA

Tamil Nadu

On a certain village of the country of Śeṅgalinîrppaṭṭu[1] there dwelt a Brâhmaṇ, gaining his living by the alms he collected daily, and so he was in extremely poor circumstances. Poverty indeed had taken such a firm hold of him that he wished to fly to Bânâras. Accordingly, depending as usual upon what charity would provide for him on the way, he started with only one day's supplies tied up in a bundle.

When there wanted yet four *ghaṭikâs* before sunset he had approached a thick wilderness, which was also long and wide, and studded with small villages here and there. After journeying through this for more than the four *ghaṭikâs* he reached a splendid tank just as the sun was setting. Ablutions must never be foregone by a Brâhmaṇ, so he neared the tank to wash his hands and legs, to perform his prayers, and to eat what little his bundle contained. As soon as he placed his foot in the water he heard a voice calling out:—"Put not thy foot in this water! Thou art not permitted to do so!"

He looked round about him and discovered nothing, and so not heeding the threat he washed his hands and feet, and sat down to perform his

---

1. Śeṅgalinîrppaṭṭu means "the land of the blue lily," now corrupted into Chingleput.

sandhyâvandana or evening worship, when again he heard a voice:—"Perform not thy *sandhyâvandana*! Thou art not permitted to do so!"

A second time he gave no heed to the voice but proceeded with his prayers, and when they were over opened his bundle of food. As soon as he began to eat the same voice was again heard, but the Brâhman paid no attention, and finished his meal. Then getting up he pursued his journey, so as, if possible, to reach a village to sleep in for the night. He had scarcely advanced a step, when again the same voice forbade him to go on!

Having thus been barred four times the Brâhman boldly broke out and said:—"Who art thou, thou wretch? And why dost thou thus forbid me every reasonable action?"

Replied a voice from a *pîpal* tree above him: "I am a *Brahmarâkshasa*, named Gânapriya.[2] In my former life I was a Brâhman, and learnt all the intricacies of music, but I was unwilling to impart my hard-earned knowledge to others. Paramêśvara was so greatly displeased with me that he made me a *Brahmarâkshasa* in this life[3] and even now his rage seems not to have been appeased. At the distance of a quarter of a *ghaṭikâ* from this spot is a ruined temple, in which *pûjâ* (worship) is conducted in a very rough way, and during the ceremony a piper plays upon a *nâgasvara* pipe so very awkwardly, that it causes me the utmost mortification to listen to him. My only hope of escape is that a Brâhman will rescue me from this tree. You are the first Brâhman I have ever met with in this wilderness, and I have grown quite thin from the worry of hearing that awkward piper day after day! If I continue much longer in this tree, it will be the death of me! So pity my condition, I beseech you, and remove me to some tree five or six *ghaṭikâs* distance from this place, and leave me in peace there, so that I may

---

2.   This means merely "lover of music."

3.   It is a common notion among Hindûs, especially among Brâhmans, that he who does not freely impart his knowledge to others is born in the next life as a kind of demon called *Brahmarâkshasa*.

be out of the reach of that horrible piper and get a little stouter. In return demand from me any boon and I will grant it."

Thus said the *Brahmarâkshasa*, and in its very voice the Brâhmaṇ could discover its failing strength. Said he:—"I am an extremely poor Brâhmaṇ, and if you promise to mend my condition and to make me rich I will remove you to a good distance, where the sound of the cracked *nâgasvara* shall never affect your ears."

The *Brahmarâkshasa* thought for a few *nimishas* and thus replied:— "Holy Brâhmaṇ, every person must undergo what is cut upon his forehead by Brahmâ, in this world. Five more years of poverty are allotted to you by fate, after which I shall go and possess the Princess of Maisûr, and none of the incantations which learned magicians may pronounce upon me shall drive me out, until you have presented yourself before the king of Maisûr and promised to cure her of me. He will promise you ample rewards, and you must commence the cure, when I will leave her. The king will be pleased and grant you several boons, which will make you happy. But you must never afterwards visit any place where I may be. It may be that I shall possess several princesses, but if you come there with the view of curing them I shall take your life at a blow. Beware!"

Thus spake the *Brahmarâkshasa*, and the Brâhmaṇ agreed to all the conditions and removed it to another *pîpal* tree seven *ghaṭikâs* distant from its then abode. It found its new home comfortable, and let the Brâhmaṇ pursue his way north to Bânâras, which he reached in six months.

For five years he lived in the Hanumanta Ghaṭṭa at Bânâras, performing ablutions to wash himself pure of all his sins. Then, thinking of the *Brahma-râkshasa*'s promise, he returned towards the south, and after travelling for five months reached Maisûr, where he sojourned in an old woman's house and enquired the news of the day.

Said she:—"My son, the princess of this country, who is the only daughter of the king, has been possessed by a furious devil for the last five months and all the exorcists of Jambûdvîpa have tried their skill on her, but to no purpose. He who cures her will become the master of a vast fortune."

So said the old woman to the secret joy of the Brâhmaṇ at the faithful observance of its promise by the *Brahmarâkshasa*. He bathed and hastily took his meal, and then presented himself at the *darbâr* that very day. The king promised him several villages and whole elephant-loads of *mohars* should he effect a cure.

On these conditions he commenced his pretended exorcisms, and on the third day asked for all the persons assembled to vacate the room in which the possessed princess was seated. Then he explained to his friend the *Brahmarâkshasa*, who was now possessing her, that he was the Brâhmaṇ who had assisted him in the wood five years previously. The demon was greatly pleased to meet its old friend again, and wishing him prosperity and warning him never to come again to any other place where it might go for shelter, took its leave. The princess came back to her former self, and the Brâhmaṇ, loaded with wealth and lands, settled down in Maisûr.

He had thus earned a name as an exorcist, and now cultivated that science secretly, so that he soon became a master of it, and all over the country he became famous as a master-magician. He also became a favourite with the king of Maisûr, and married a beautiful Brâhmaṇî girl by whom he became the father of three children. Thus passed full ten years.

Meanwhile the *Brahmarâkshasa*, after going to several places, went to the country of Tiruvanandapuram (Trivandrum) and possessed the Princess of Travancore. Many masters of magic were called in, but to no effect. At length rumours about the master-magician of Maisûr reached the ears of the king of Tiruvanandapuram. He at once wrote to the Mahârâja of Maisûr, who showed the letter to the Brâhmaṇ. The invitation was a death stroke to our hero; for if he refused to go he would lose his good name and the favour of his king, and if he went he would lose his life! He preferred the latter alternative, and at once wrote out a *will*, leaving his estate to his children and confiding them to careful hands. He then started from Maisûr for Tiruvanandapuram, which he reached after journeying for a month. The king had so arranged for his comfort that he performed the journey with apparent ease: but his heart beating painfully!

He reached Tiruvanandapuram and tried to postpone his exorcisms for this reason or that for a short time, but the king was determined to prove him. So he was asked to leave no stone unturned in order to effect the perfect cure of the princess. He had now no hope in this world, and thinking that his days were numbered he undertook the cure. As usual he made a pretence for a few days with his incantations, but he thought: "After all, what is the use of my thus prolonging my miseries, as it is settled that I must die? The sooner there is an end to them the better!" So with a determined will to fall before the blow of the *Brahmarâkshasa* he entered the chamber in which the princess was seated, but just as he entered a thought came into his mind and he said boldly:—"Will you now abandon her, you *Brahmarâkshasa*, or shall I at once bring in the piper of the ruined temple near the wood, who is waiting outside?"

No sooner had the name of the awkward piper fallen on the ears of the *Brahmarâkshasa*, than he threw down the long pole, which he had in his hand to thrash the Brâhmaṇ with, and fell at his feet, saying:—

"Brother Brâhmaṇ, I will never even look back, but run away at once, if you will only never bring that piper to me again!"

"Agreed," said our hero, and Gâṇapriya disappeared.

Of course, our hero was greatly rewarded for his success and became doubly famous throughout the world as a master-magician!

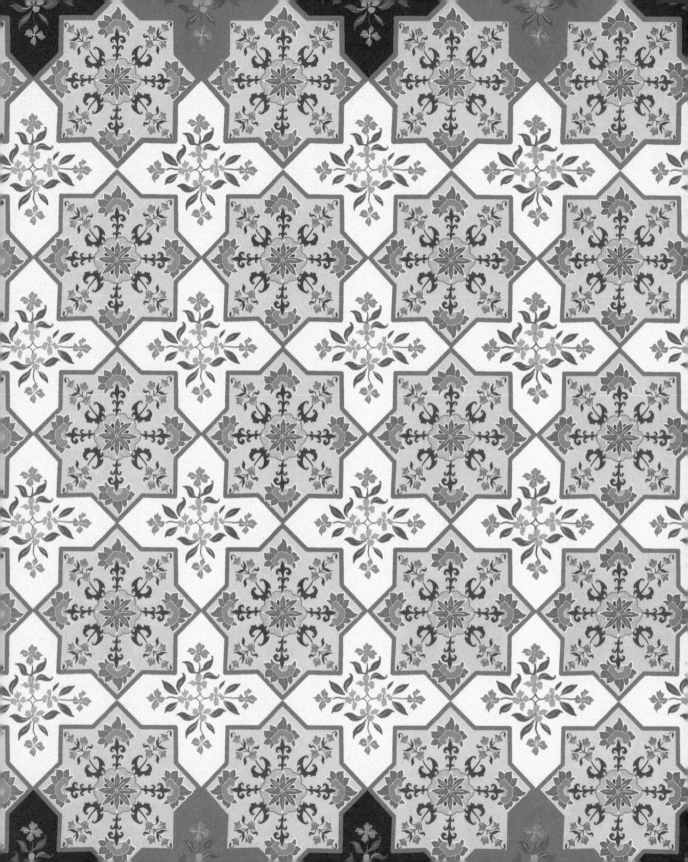

Life and Death

LIFE'S SECRET

❖ ┄•❈•┄ ❖

Bengal

There was a king who had two queens, Duo and Suo.[1] Both of them were childless. One day a Faquir (mendicant) came to the palace-gate to ask for alms. The Suo queen went to the door with a handful of rice. The mendicant asked whether she had any children. On being answered in the negative, the holy mendicant refused to take alms, as the hands of a woman unblessed with child are regarded as ceremonially unclean. He offered her a drug for removing her barrenness, and she expressing her willingness to receive it, he gave it to her with the following directions:—"Take this nostrum, swallow it with the juice of the pomegranate flower; if you do this, you will have a son in due time. The son will be exceedingly handsome, and his complexion will be of the colour of the pomegranate flower; and you shall call him Dalim Kumar.[2] As enemies will try to take away the life of your son, I may as well tell you that the life of the boy will be bound up in the life of a big *boal* fish which is in your tank, in front of the palace. In the heart of the fish is a small box of wood, in the box is a necklace of gold, that necklace is the life of your son. Farewell."

---

1. Kings, in Bengali folk-tales, have invariably two queens—the elder is called *duo*, that is, not loved; and the younger is called *suo*, that is, loved.

2. *Dalim* or *dadimba* means a pomegranate, and *kumara* son.

In the course of a month or so it was whispered in the palace that the Suo queen had hopes of an heir. Great was the joy of the king. Visions of an heir to the throne, and of a never-ending succession of powerful monarchs perpetuating his dynasty to the latest generations, floated before his mind, and made him glad as he had never been in his life. The usual ceremonies performed on such occasions were celebrated with great pomp; and the subjects made loud demonstrations of their joy at the anticipation of so auspicious an event as the birth of a prince. In the fulness of time the Suo queen gave birth to a son of uncommon beauty. When the king the first time saw the face of the infant, his heart leaped with joy. The ceremony of the child's first rice was celebrated with extraordinary pomp, and the whole kingdom was filled with gladness.

In course of time Dalim Kumar grew up a fine boy. Of all sports he was most addicted to playing with pigeons. This brought him into frequent contact with his stepmother, the Duo queen, into whose apartments Dalim's pigeons had a trick of always flying. The first time the pigeons flew into her rooms, she readily gave them up to the owner; but the second time she gave them up with some reluctance. The fact is that the Duo queen, perceiving that Dalim's pigeons had this happy knack of flying into her apartments, wished to take advantage of it for the furtherance of her own selfish views. She naturally hated the child, as the king, since his birth, neglected her more than ever, and idolised the fortunate mother of Dalim. She had heard, it is not known how, that the holy mendicant that had given the famous pill to the Suo queen had also told her of a secret connected with the child's life. She had heard that the child's life was bound up with something—she did not know with what. She determined to extort that secret from the boy. Accordingly, the next time the pigeons flew into her rooms, she refused to give them up, addressing the child thus:—"I won't give the pigeons up unless you tell me one thing."

Dalim.—What thing, mamma?

Duo.—Nothing particular, my darling; I only want to know in what your life is.

Dalim.—What is that, mamma? Where can my life be except in me?

Duo.—No, child; that is not what I mean. A holy mendicant told your mother that your life is bound up with something. I wish to know what that thing is.

Dalim.—I never heard of any such thing, mamma.

Duo.—If you promise to inquire of your mother in what thing your life is, and if you tell me what your mother says, then I will let you have the pigeons, otherwise not.

Dalim.—Very well, I'll inquire, and let you know. Now, please, give me my pigeons.

Duo.—I'll give them on one condition more. Promise to me that you will not tell your mother that I want the information.

Dalim.—I promise.

The Duo queen let go the pigeons, and Dalim, overjoyed to find again his beloved birds, forgot every syllable of the conversation he had had with his stepmother. The next day, however, the pigeons again flew into the Duo queen's rooms. Dalim went to his stepmother, who asked him for the required information. The boy promised to ask his mother that very day, and begged hard for the release of the pigeons. The pigeons were at last delivered. After play, Dalim went to his mother and said—"Mamma, please tell me in what my life is contained." "What do you mean, child?" asked the mother, astonished beyond measure at the child's extraordinary question. "Yes, Mamma," rejoined the child, "I have heard that a holy mendicant told you that my life is contained in something. Tell me what that thing is." "My pet, my darling, my treasure, my golden-moon, do not ask such an inauspicious question. Let the mouth of my enemies be covered with ashes, and let my Dalim live for ever," said the mother, earnestly. But the child insisted on being informed of the secret. He said he would not eat or drink anything unless the information were given him. The Suo queen, pressed by the importunity of her son, in an evil hour told the child the secret of his life. The next day the pigeons again, as fate would have it, flew into the Duo queen's rooms. Dalim went for them; the stepmother plied the boy with sugared words, and obtained the knowledge of the secret.

The Duo queen, on learning the secret of Dalim Kumar's life, lost no time in using it for the prosecution of her malicious design. She told her maid-servants to get for her some dried stalks of the hemp plant, which are very brittle, and which, when pressed upon, make a peculiar noise, not unlike the cracking of joints of bones in the human body. These hemp stalks she put under her bed, upon which she laid herself down and gave out that she was dangerously ill. The king, though he did not love her so well as his other queen, was in duty bound to visit her in her illness. The queen pretended that her bones were all cracking; and sure enough, when she tossed from one side of her bed to the other, the hemp stalks made the noise wanted. The king, believing that the Duo queen was seriously ill, ordered his best physician to attend her. With that physician the Duo queen was in collusion. The physician said to the king that for the queen's complaint there was but one remedy, which consisted in the outward application of something to be found inside a large *boal* fish which was in the tank before the palace. The king's fisherman was accordingly called and ordered to catch the *boal* in question. On the first throw of the net the fish was caught. It so happened that Dalim Kumar, along with other boys, was playing not far from the tank. The moment the *boal* fish was caught in the net, that moment Dalim felt unwell; and when the fish was brought up to land, Dalim fell down on the ground, and made as if he was about to breathe his last. He was immediately taken into his mother's room, and the king was astonished on hearing of the sudden illness of his son and heir. The fish was by the order of the physician taken into the room of the Duo queen, and as it lay on the floor striking its fins on the ground, Dalim in his mother's room was given up for lost. When the fish was cut open, a casket was found in it; and in the casket lay a necklace of gold. The moment the necklace was worn by the queen, that very moment Dalim died in his mother's room.

When the news of the death of his son and heir reached the king he was plunged into an ocean of grief, which was not lessened in any degree by the intelligence of the recovery of the Duo queen. He wept over his dead Dalim so bitterly that his courtiers were apprehensive of a permanent derangement of his mental powers. The king would not allow the dead body of his son to be either buried or burnt. He could not realise the fact of his son's death; it was so entirely causeless and so terribly sudden. He ordered the dead body to be removed to one of his garden-houses in the suburbs of the city, and to be laid there in state. He ordered that all sorts of provisions should be stowed away in that house, as if the young prince needed them for his refection. Orders were issued that the house should be kept locked up day and night, and that no one should go into it except Dalim's most intimate friend, the son of the king's prime minister, who was intrusted with the key of the house, and who obtained the privilege of entering it once in twenty-four hours.

As, owing to her great loss, the Suo queen lived in retirement, the king gave up his nights entirely to the Duo queen. The latter, in order to allay suspicion, used to put aside the gold necklace at night; and, as fate had ordained that Dalim should be in the state of death only during the time that the necklace was round the neck of the queen, he passed into the state of life whenever the necklace was laid aside. Accordingly Dalim revived every night, as the Duo queen every night put away the necklace, and died again the next morning when the queen put it on. When Dalim became re-animated at night he ate whatever food he liked, for of such there was a plentiful stock in the garden-house, walked about on the premises, and meditated on the singularity of his lot. Dalim's friend, who visited him only during the day, found him always lying a lifeless corpse; but what struck him after some days was the singular fact that the body remained in the same state in which he saw it on the first day of his visit. There was no sign of putrefaction. Except that it was lifeless and pale, there were no symptoms of corruption—it was apparently quite fresh. Unable to account for so strange a phenomenon, he determined to watch the corpse more closely, and to visit it not only during the day but sometimes also at night. The first night that he paid his visit he was astounded to see his dead friend sauntering about in the garden. At first he thought the figure might be only the ghost of his friend, but on feeling him and otherwise examining him, he found the apparition to be veritable flesh and blood. Dalim related to his friend all the circumstances connected with his death; and they both concluded that he revived at nights only because the Duo queen put aside her necklace when the king visited her. As the life of the prince depended on the necklace, the two friends laid their heads together to devise if possible some plans by which they might get possession of it. Night after night they consulted together, but they could not think of any feasible scheme. At length the gods brought about the deliverance of Dalim Kumar in a wonderful manner.

Some years before the time of which we are speaking, the sister of Bidhata-Purusha[3] was delivered of a daughter. The anxious mother asked her brother what he had written on her child's forehead; to which Bidhata-Purusha replied that she should get married to a dead bridegroom. Maddened as she became with grief at the prospect of such a dreary destiny for her daughter, she yet thought it useless to remonstrate with her brother, for she well knew that he never changed what he once wrote. As the child grew in years she became exceedingly beautiful, but the mother could not

---

3.   Bidhata-Purusha is the deity that predetermines all the events of the life of man or woman, and writes on the forehead of the child, on the sixth day of its birth, a brief *precis* of them.

look upon her with pleasure in consequence of the portion allotted to her by her divine brother. When the girl came to marriageable age, the mother resolved to flee from the country with her, and thus avert her dreadful destiny. But the decrees of fate cannot thus be overruled. In the course of their wanderings the mother and daughter arrived at the gate of that very garden-house in which Dalim Kumar lay. It was evening. The girl said she was thirsty and wanted to drink water. The mother told her daughter to sit at the gate, while she went to search for drinking water in some neighbouring hut. In the meantime the girl through curiosity pushed the door of the garden-house, which opened of itself. She then went in and saw a beautiful palace, and was wishing to come out when the door shut itself of its own accord, so that she could not get out. As night came on the prince revived, and, walking about, saw a human figure near the gate. He went up to it, and found it was a girl of surpassing beauty. On being asked who she was, she told Dalim Kumar all the details of her little history,—how her uncle, the divine Bidhata-Purusha, wrote on her forehead at her birth that she should get married to a dead bridegroom, how her mother had no pleasure in her life at the prospect of so terrible a destiny, and how, therefore, on the approach of her womanhood, with a view to avert so dreadful a catastrophe, she had left her house with her and wandered in various places, how they came to the gate of the garden-house, and how her mother had now gone in search of drinking water for her. Dalim Kumar, hearing her simple and pathetic story, said, "I am the dead bridegroom, and you must get married to me, come with me to the house." "How can you be said to be a dead bridegroom when you are standing and speaking to me?" said the girl. "You will understand it afterwards," rejoined the prince, "come now and follow me." The girl followed the prince into the house. As she had been fasting the whole day the prince hospitably entertained her. As for the mother of the girl, the sister of the divine Bidhata-Purusha, she returned to the gate of the garden-house after it was dark, cried out for her daughter, and getting no answer, went away in search of her in the huts in the neighbourhood. It is said that after this she was not seen anywhere.

While the niece of the divine Bidhata-Purusha was partaking of the hospitality of Dalim Kumar, his friend as usual made his appearance. He was surprised not a little at the sight of the fair stranger; and his surprise became greater when he heard the story of the young lady from her own lips. It was forthwith resolved that very night to unite the young couple in the bonds of matrimony. As priests were out of the question, the hymeneal rites were performed *à la Gandharva*.[4] The friend of the bridegroom took leave of the newly-married couple and went away to his house. As the happy pair had spent the greater part of the night in wakefulness, it was long after sunrise that they awoke from their sleep;—I should have said that the young wife woke from her sleep, for the prince had become a cold corpse, life having departed from him. The feelings of the young wife may be easily imagined. She shook her husband, imprinted warm kisses on his cold lips, but in vain. He was as lifeless as a marble statue. Stricken with horror, she smote her breast, struck her forehead with the palms of her hands, tore her hair and went about in the house and in the garden as if she had gone mad. Dalim's friend did not come into the house during the day, as he deemed it improper to pay a visit to her while her husband was lying dead. The day seemed to the poor girl as long as a year, but the longest day has its end, and when the shades of evening were descending upon the landscape, her dead husband was awakened into consciousness; he rose up from his bed, embraced his disconsolate wife, ate, drank, and became merry. His friend made his appearance as usual, and the whole night was spent in gaiety and festivity. Amid this alternation of life and

---

4. There are eight forms of marriage spoken of in the Hindu Sastras, of which the Gandharva is one, consisting in the exchange of garlands.

death did the prince and his lady spend some seven or eight years, during which time the princess presented her husband with two lovely boys who were the exact image of their father.

It is superfluous to remark that the king, the two queens, and other members of the royal household did not know that Dalim Kumar was living, at any rate, was living at night. They all thought that he was long ago dead and his corpse burnt. But the heart of Dalim's wife was yearning after her mother-in-law, whom she had never seen. She conceived a plan by which she might be able not only to have a sight of her mother-in-law, but also to get hold of the Duo queen's necklace, on which her husband's life was dependent. With the consent of her husband and of his friend she disguised herself as a female barber. Like every female barber she took a bundle containing the following articles:—an iron instrument for paring nails, another iron instrument for scraping off the superfluous flesh of the soles of the feet, a piece of *jhama* or burnt brick for rubbing the soles of the feet with, and *alakta*[5] for painting the edges of the feet and toes with. Taking this bundle in her hand she stood at the gate of the king's palace with her two boys. She declared herself to be a barber, and expressed a desire to see the Suo queen, who readily gave her an interview. The queen was quite taken up with the two little boys, who, she declared, strongly reminded her of her darling Dalim Kumar. Tears fell profusely from her eyes at the recollection of her lost treasure; but she of course had not the remotest idea that the two little boys were the sons of her own dear Dalim. She told the supposed barber that she did not require her services, as, since the death of her son, she had given up all terrestrial vanities, and among others the practice of dyeing her feet red; but she added that, nevertheless, she would be glad now and then to see her and her two fine boys. The

---

5. *Alakta* is leaves or flimsy paper saturated with lac.

female barber, for so we must now call her, then went to the quarters of the Duo queen and offered her services. The queen allowed her to pare her nails, to scrape off the superfluous flesh of her feet, and to paint them with *alakta* and was so pleased with her skill, and the sweetness of her disposition, that she ordered her to wait upon her periodically. The female barber noticed with no little concern the necklace round the queen's neck. The day of her second visit came on, and she instructed the elder of her two sons to set up a loud cry in the palace, and not to stop crying till he got into his hands the Duo queen's necklace. The female barber, accordingly, went again on the appointed day to the Duo queen's apartments. While she was engaged in painting the queen's feet, the elder boy set up a loud cry. On being asked the reason of the cry, the boy, as previously instructed, said that he wanted the queen's necklace. The queen said that it was impossible for her to part with that particular necklace, for it was the best and most valuable of all her jewels. To gratify the boy, however, she took it off her neck, and put it into the boy's hand. The boy stopped crying and held the necklace tight in his hand. As the female barber after she had done her work was about to go away, the queen wanted the necklace back. But the boy would not part with it. When his mother attempted to snatch it from him, he wept bitterly, and showed as if his heart would break. On which the female barber said—"Will your Majesty be gracious enough to let the boy take the necklace home with him? When he falls asleep after drinking his milk, which he is sure to do in the course of an hour, I will carefully bring it back to you." The queen, seeing that the boy would not allow it to be taken away from him, agreed to the proposal of the female barber, especially reflecting that Dalim, whose life depended on it, had long ago gone to the abodes of death.

Thus possessed of the treasure on which the life of her husband depended, the woman went with breathless haste to the garden-house and presented the necklace to Dalim, who had been restored to life. Their joy knew no bounds, and by the advice of their friend they determined the next day to go to the palace in state, and present themselves to the king and the Suo queen. Due preparations were made; an elephant, richly caparisoned, was brought for the prince Dalim Kumar, a pair of ponies for the two little boys, and a *chaturdala*[6] furnished with curtains of gold lace for the princess. Word was sent to the king and the Suo queen that the prince Dalim Kumar was not only alive, but that he was coming to visit his royal parents with his wife and sons. The king and Suo queen could hardly believe in the report, but being assured of its truth they were entranced with joy; while the Duo queen, anticipating the disclosure of all her wiles, became overwhelmed with grief. The procession of Dalim Kumar, which was attended by a band of musicians, approached the palace-gate; and the king and Suo queen went out to receive their long-lost son. It is needless to say that their joy was intense. They fell on each other's neck and wept. Dalim then related all the circumstances connected with his death. The king, inflamed with rage, ordered the Duo queen into his presence. A large hole, as deep as the height of a man, was dug in the ground. The Duo queen was put into it in a standing posture. Prickly thorn was heaped around her up to the crown of her head; and in this manner she was buried alive.

Thus my story endeth,

The Natiya-thorn withereth;

"Why, O Natiya-thorn, dost wither?"

"Why does thy cow on me browse?"

"Why, O cow, dost thou browse?"

"Why does thy neat-herd not tend me?"

"Why, O neat-herd, dost not tend the cow?"

---

6.   A sort of open *Palki*, used generally for carrying the bridegroom and bride in marriage processions.

"Why does thy daughter-in-law not give me rice?"

"Why, O daughter-in-law, dost not give rice?"

"Why does my child cry?"

"Why, O child, dost thou cry?"

"Why does the ant bite me?"

"Why, O ant, dost thou bite?"

Koot! koot! koot!

EESARA
and CANEESARA

> ···✿···

Punjab

Some years ago there lived two merchants, a Hindoo and a Mahomedan, who were partners in the same business. The name of the Hindoo was Eesara, and the name of the Mahomedan was Caneesara. They had once been extremely well off, but hard times had come upon them, and their business had declined, and they had gradually sunk into poverty.

One day Caneesara came to the house of Eesara and said: "Lend us something—some money, or some grain, or some bread—we have absolutely nothing to eat."

"O friend," answered Eesara, "you are not in worse plight than we are. We are quite destitute of everything. What can I give you?"

So Caneesara's visit was fruitless, and he returned empty-handed as he had come.

After he had gone, Eesara said to his wife: "All we have is a brass plate and a single brass cup. As the plate is of value, put it for safety into a net and hang it from the roof over our beds; and put some water in the plate, so that if Caneesara comes into the house to steal it when we are asleep, the water will spill on our faces and we shall awake."

That very night Caneesara, who knew of the brass plate, determined to make an effort to become possessed of it. So, long after the inmates were in bed, he visited the house of Eesara, and, softly lifting the latch, stole into the apartment. There, in the faint light of the moon, he saw the plate hanging in a net over the beds, but, being a cunning fellow and suspecting a trick, he first put his forefinger through the net and discovered that the plate contained water. To avoid detection, he now took up some sand, and, with the utmost care, dropped it gradually into the plate, until the whole of the water was absorbed. Having accomplished this, he slowly abstracted the plate from the net and made off with it.

On his way home he considered that his wisest course would be to hide the plate for a short time until he met with an opportunity of selling it. Going, therefore, to a tank, he waded into it some distance, and buried it in the mud, and in order to mark the place he stuck in a long reed which he had plucked on the margin. Then, perfectly satisfied with his success, he went home and got into bed.

The next morning, when Eesara awoke, he missed the plate, and cried: "O wife, Caneesara has been here. He has stolen the plate."

Going at once to his friend's house, he searched it high and low, but returned home no wiser than he was before. As the day was far spent, he went out to the tank for his accustomed bath. When he arrived at the edge of the water, he observed the solitary reed nodding in the wind, and said: "Hallo! this was not here yesterday. This is some trick of Caneesara's." So he waded into the water, and had the satisfaction of discovering his missing plate, which he carried home to his wife, but he left the tell-tale reed undisturbed.

After a day or two Caneesara came down to the tank, and wading out to his reed, began to grope among the mud for the brass plate, but he groped in vain. "Ah!" groaned he, "Eesara has been here." Vexed and disappointed, he returned to his house and smoked his hookah.

Caneesara now visited his partner once more, and said to him: "Friend Eesara, we are both as badly off as we can be. Let us now go together to some other country, and let us take our account-books with us, and see if by hook or by crook we cannot make some money." To this proposal Eesara agreed, and the two friends set out on their travels.

After a weary tramp they arrived at a city in which a rich merchant had recently died, and by inquiry they found that, his body having been burnt, his remains had been duly laid in a certain place. Then Eesara, by tampering with the ledgers which he had brought with him from his own home, concocted a tremendous bill against the defunct merchant, ingeniously running up the amount to forty thousand rupees. When night set in, the two friends went to the place of sepulture, and dug out a chamber, in which Caneesara hid himself, while Eesara covered him over with sticks and earth, and, in short, managed his task so well that in the morning no one would have suspected that the ground had been disturbed at all. Eesara, armed with his account-books, went presently to the house of the sons of the dead merchant, and said to them: "Both your father and your grandfather were in debt to the house of which I am a partner. The total sum due to us is forty thousand rupees, and payment is requested without more delay."

The sons at first attempted to brave it out. "Not a farthing do we owe you," said they. "Why was not this monstrous claim sent in before?"

"The claim is true," replied Eesara, "and the money is owing in full. I appeal to your dead father. Let him be the judge. I cite you to appear with me at his grave."

The two sons, thus solemnly charged, accompanied their pretended creditor to their father's grave. Now, the dead man's name was Bahnooshâh.

"O Bahnooshâh," cried Eesara, "thou model of honour and probity, hear and answer! Are you indebted in the sum of forty thousand rupees to the house of Eesara and Caneesara, or are you not?"

Three times was this appeal made with a loud voice over the grave, and in answer to the third appeal Caneesara spoke in a sepulchral tone from the bowels of the earth: "Oh, my sons," cried he, "if you are faithful to my memory, leave not this weight of woe on my soul, but pay the money at once."

The sons were overwhelmed, and, dropping on their knees, promised to fulfil the request of the dead. They then returned home, and taking Eesara into their counting-house, paid him over the sum demanded, and presented him with a mule in addition to carry away the burden. Eesara, who was beyond measure enchanted with the success of his stratagem, forgot in the full flow of his happiness to return for his partner, and having mounted the mule and ensconced himself in comfort between the saddle-bags, he made haste to get out of the town.

By this time Caneesara, beginning to tire of being pent up in his dark, narrow lodging, was thinking to himself: "Strange! Why does not Eesara come back with news?" And, unable to bear the suspense any longer, he burst open his frail tenement and entered the town. Going to the house of the deluded merchants, he inquired for one named Eesara, and learnt that he had just received the amount of the debt, and had departed. "There he goes," said they, "on yonder mule." Following with his eyes the direction indicated, he saw Eesara astride of the mule going up a neighbouring hill, and occasionally belabouring his stubborn animal with a cudgel. "Ha! ha!" laughed Caneesara, "so Eesara is leaving me in the lurch." And he began to follow him.

Now, as Eesara jogged along he saw a handsome gold-embroidered shoe lying upon the road; but he was too proud in the possession of his newly-acquired wealth to regard such a trifle as an odd shoe, however embroidered, and he continued his way without dismounting. When Caneesara arrived at the spot, however, he picked up the shoe, and a happy thought striking him, he ran at the top of his speed round by some rocks along a by-way and joined the main track again some distance ahead of Eesara. There he laid down the shoe in the middle of the road, and hid himself in a bush.

Eesara, riding up as happy as a king, turned a projecting corner of the road and at once espied the shoe. Reining up his mule, he gazed at it and cried: "Ha! here's the fellow of the shoe I left behind—the same pattern and everything." And, dismounting, he picked up the shoe, tied his mule to the very bush in which Caneesara was in hiding, and ran back as hard as he could go for the supposed fellow. The moment he was out of sight Caneesara got down from the bush, mounted the mule, and rode off at a full pace.

Now, Eesara, of course, looked for the fellow-shoe in vain, and, what was still harder to bear, he returned to the bush to find his mule gone. "Ha!" said he, "Caneesara has been here!" And he hastened on foot towards his own village.

Meanwhile Caneesara was also pressing on with all speed. He arrived at his home in the middle of the night, and without a word to any of his neighbours he unloaded the mule and drove it away into the forest. He then summoned his wife, and the two between them carried the bags of money into the house and buried them under the mud floor. But being afraid of unpleasant questions if he met Eesara just then, he absented himself from home, charging his wife not to reveal the fact of his arrival.

Eesara, by no means despairing, arrived at his own house and related his adventures to his wife, who agreed with him in his opinion that the money had been taken by Caneesara. "And what is more," said Eesara, "he has buried it in his house."

The next night the wife of Eesara invited the wife of Caneesara to spend a few hours with her, and during the interval Eesara visited the house of his partner and successfully dug up the money, after which he restored the floor to its former appearance. Taking the hoard to his own house, which he entered after the departure of Caneesara's wife, he buried it in like manner under the floor of his chamber. He then went off and hid himself in an old dry well, directing his wife to bring him his food at a certain hour every day.

By this time Caneesara had ventured to return to his home, and choosing a proper time for the purpose, he dug up the floor of his house, stopping now and then to chuckle with his wife over the success of his stratagem. But, alas! the money was nowhere to be found, and he laboured in vain. "Ha!" cried he, throwing down his spade, "Eesara has been here!" Then he considered within himself, "Eesara has taken away the money, but instead of looking for the money I shall now look for Eesara himself."

Caneesara now watched in the neighbourhood of Eesara's house night and day, and observing that his wife always went out at the same hour, he began to suspect that she must be taking her husband's food somewhere. So he dogged her footsteps at a safe distance, and discovered that she made for the old well. There he watched her from behind a boulder, and saw her take bread and buttermilk from under her veil, and lower the food with a piece of string down the well. After a time he noticed that she drew up the empty vessel, and, with a few words to the person below, returned to the town. "Ha, ha!" laughed Caneesara, "Eesara is here; he is down that well! But where can the money be?"

That night Caneesara made up some atrociously bad bread, and the next day he disguised himself as a woman in a long red cloth, and taking with him the bread, a vessel, and a piece of string, he went out to the well and lowered down the food.

"Oh, you cursed woman!" cried Eesara in a rage, "what bread is this you have brought me?"

"O husband!" answered Caneesara in feigned tones, "you rail at your poor wife, but what am I to do without money?"

"You wretched woman!" said Eesara, "you know that under the floor of our old house there are bags and bags of money! Why can't you take a rupee occasionally and buy me decent victuals?"

Caneesara, having heard quite enough for his purpose pulled up the empty vessel and took himself off. He passed the real wife on his way into town, and going straight to the house, he abstracted the whole of the money, and carried it to his own house; but this time he buried it in the garden.

Meanwhile, Eesara's wife, having arrived at the well, let down her husband's food. Eesara, when he saw the suspended vessel again bobbing in front of him, cried out: "Hullo! you here again? It is not half an hour since you were here before!"

"What are you talking about?" answered the woman. "I have not been near you since this time yesterday."

"Ah!" exclaimed Eesara with a groan, "is that so? Then Caneesara has been here, and we are undone again!"

So he climbed up by the loose masonry and came out of the well. "Now let us go home," said he, "and look after the money." When he came to his house it was too evident that the place had been rifled, and having plied his shovel to no purpose, he rushed off to the house of Caneesara. His wily partner, however, was nowhere to be found, nor with all his searching and digging could he light on the slightest trace of the lost treasure. At last, baffled and disappointed, he went back to his wife and got her to lay him out as if he were dead, and to bewail him after the custom of his people. Then came the neighbours bearing bundles of wood, and a funeral-pyre was erected to burn his body. Caneesara, hearing of these lugubrious preparations, said to himself: "All this, I fear, is only some trick of my old friend;" and he went to the house and asked permission to view the body. "This merchant who is dead was a friend of mine," said he. But they drove him out of the place, saying: "No, no; you are a Mahomedan."

Eesara was now carried out of the house on a stretcher and laid on the top of the funeral-pyre, while blankets and clothes were held round to keep off the gaze of the multitude. Just as the torches were applied, and the smoke began to envelop him, and while the confusion was at its height, he slipped out of his shroud, and, taking advantage of the darkness, he managed to escape from the scene unobserved. His first act was to go again to the house of Caneesara, feeling satisfied that he must by that time have ventured to return; but the latter, full of suspicion and in dread of his life, still kept out of the way. So Eesara's search was a complete failure. "I cannot find the money," said he; "but Caneesara I am determined to hunt out, and then we shall have an account to settle."

Caneesara now resolved to feign death in his turn. "Eesara has not deceived me," said he; "but if I can deceive Eesara, I will return some night, dig up the money, and be off to other parts." So first of all a rumour was circulated that he was very ill; then it was asserted that he was dead; and his wife, to keep up the deceit, laid him out and bewailed him with shrieks and moaning cries. When the neighbours came about, they said: "Alas! it is poor Caneesara!" And they ordered his shroud and carried his body to the grave. There they laid it down upon the earth, close by the tomb of an old hermit, for the customary observances, and Eesara, who had followed the mourners, contrived to get a peep at his friend's face, saying: "This poor man, as you know, was a crony of mine." Having satisfied his doubts, he climbed into a tree, which was near the grave, and waited there until, the rites being completed, the body was laid in its chamber. As soon as the company had dispersed, night having now set in, Eesara got down from the tree, crept to the old tomb, and, lifting up the slab, dragged out the body alive and laid it down by the edge of the grave. Just then the noise of approaching footsteps and subdued whispers caught his attention, and he again got into the tree, wondering what this interruption could be.

The party which now approached was a gang of notorious robbers, seven in number, one of whom was blind of an eye. Catching sight of the body in the old tomb, they examined it with great care, and exclaimed: "See, this must be some famous saint! He has come out of his grave, and his body is perfectly fresh. Let us pray to him for favour and good luck!" So they one and all fell down on their knees and besought his assistance. "We are pledged to a robbery this night," said they. "If we are successful, O saint, into your mouth we shall drop some sugar." The one-eyed man, however, said: "As for me, I shall tickle his throat with some water."

Having made their vows, they all set out for the town, robbed a rich man's house, and returned, each one bearing his own bag of money, to the graveyard. They now dropped morsels of sugar into Caneesara's mouth in accordance with their promises; but when it came to the turn of the robber of the one eye, he dropped in some vile water. Poor Caneesara had accepted the sugar with stolid indifference; but the water, tickling his gullet, nearly choked him, and he began to cough most violently. Precisely at this moment Eesara, who had been an absorbed observer of the scene, suddenly shrieked out in menacing tones: "Never mind the fellows behind; catch the rascal who is standing in front!"

These unexpected words sounded in the robbers' ears like the voice of the black angel, and imagining themselves in the midst of evil spirits, they took to their heels and incontinently ran away, leaving their bags of money behind them by the open grave.

The dead Caneesara now sprang to his feet, crying out: "Ha! ha! Eesara is here, and I have caught him at last!" And as the latter had descended from the tree, the two friends embraced each other most cordially. Picking up the seven bags of gold, they entered the old tomb, where they managed to light one of the little earthenware lamps belonging to the shrine, and by dint of drawing the feeble flame close enough, they poured out the glittering heaps, and proceeded to settle their accounts. They were, however, unable to agree about a balance of a single farthing; and their words began to run high, each of them asserting his claim with tremendous warmth.

By this time the robbers, having come to a halt, deputed their one-eyed companion to return and look for the money. One-eyed men are proverbially cunning, and this one was determined not to impair his reputation. Creeping quietly along, he arrived at the tomb as the dispute was in full career; but, alas! he was seen; and just as his head appeared through one of the holes in the wall, Caneesara suddenly snatched off the fellow's turban, and, handing it to Eesara, cried, "Here, then, is your farthing; so now we are quits!" The robber, drawing back his head with the utmost despatch, ran as fast as his legs could carry him to his confederates, and told them: "The number of demons in that old tomb is so immense that the share of each of them comes to only a single farthing! Let us get away, or we shall all be caught and hanged!" So, in a great fright, they left the place on the instant, and never returned again.

Then said the wily Caneesara to the wily Eesara: "With the forty thousand rupees which I possess already, my share of this capture is one bag, and these other six bags are therefore yours."

The two friends were now equally rich; and returning to their homes, they bought lands and houses, and defied poverty for the rest of their days, living together with their wives and children in the utmost happiness and in the enjoyment of every blessing.

THE
LORD of DEATH

Punjab

Once upon a time there was a road, and every one who travelled along it died. Some folk said they were killed by a snake, others said by a scorpion, but certain it is they all died.

Now a very old man was travelling along the road, and being tired, sat down on a stone to rest; when suddenly, close beside him, he saw a scorpion as big as a cock, which, while he looked at it, changed into a horrible snake. He was wonderstruck, and as the creature glided away, he determined to follow it at a little distance, and so find out what it really was.

So the snake sped on day and night, and behind it followed the old man like a shadow. Once it went into an inn, and killed several travellers; another time it slid into the King's house and killed him. Then it crept up the waterspout to the Queen's palace, and killed the King's youngest daughter. So it passed on, and wherever it went the sound of weeping and wailing arose, and the old man followed it, silent as a shadow.

Suddenly the road became a broad, deep, swift river, on the banks of which sat some poor travellers who longed to cross over, but had no money to pay the ferry. Then the snake changed into a handsome buffalo, with a brass necklace and bells round its neck, and stood by the brink of the stream. When the poor travellers saw this, they said, "This beast is going to swim to its home across the river; let us get on its back, and hold on to its tail, so that we too shall get over the stream."

Then they climbed on its back and held by its tail, and the buffalo swam away with them bravely; but when it reached the middle, it began to kick, until they tumbled off, or let go, and were all drowned.

When the old man, who had crossed the river in a boat, reached the other side, the buffalo had disappeared, and in its stead stood a beautiful ox. Seeing this handsome creature wandering about, a peasant, struck with covetousness, lured it to his home. It was very gentle, suffering itself to be tied up with the other cattle; but in the dead of night it changed into a snake, bit all the flocks and herds, and then, creeping into the house, killed all the sleeping folk, and crept away. But behind it the old man still followed, as silent as a shadow.

Presently they came to another river, where the snake changed itself into the likeness of a beautiful young girl, fair to see, and covered with costly jewels. After a while, two brothers, soldiers, came by, and as they approached the girl, she began to weep bitterly.

"What is the matter?" asked the brothers; "and why do you, so young and beautiful, sit by the river alone?"

Then the snake-girl answered, "My husband was even now taking me home; and going down to the stream to look for the ferry-boat, fell to washing his face, when he slipped in, and was drowned. So I have neither husband nor relations!"

"Do not fear!" cried the elder of the two brothers, who had become enamoured of her beauty; "come with me, and I will marry you."

"On one condition," answered the girl: "you must never ask me to do any household work; and no matter for what I ask, you must give it me."

"I will obey you like a slave!" promised the young man.

"Then go at once to the well, and fetch me a cup of water. Your brother can stay with me," quoth the girl.

But when the elder brother had gone, the snake-girl turned to the younger, saying, "Fly with me, for I love you! My promise to your brother was a trick to get him away!"

"Not so!" returned the young man; "you are his promised wife, and I look on you as my sister."

On this the girl became angry, weeping and wailing, until the elder brother returned, when she called out, "O husband, what a villain is here! Your brother asked me to fly with him, and leave you!"

Then bitter wrath at this treachery arose in the elder brother's heart, so that he drew his sword and challenged the younger to battle. Then they fought all day long, until by evening they both lay dead upon the field, and then the girl took the form of a snake once more, and behind it followed the old man silent as a shadow. But at last it changed into the likeness of an old white-bearded man, and when he who had followed so long saw one like himself, he took courage, and laying hold of the white beard, asked, "Who and what are you?"

Then the old man smiled and answered, "Some call me the Lord of Death, because I go about bringing death to the world."

"Give me death!" pleaded the other, "for I have followed you far, silent as a shadow, and I am aweary."

But the Lord of Death shook his head, saying, "Not so! I only give to those whose years are full, and you have sixty years of life to come!"

Then the old white-bearded man vanished, but whether he really was the Lord of Death, or a devil, who can tell?

PRINCE LIONHEART
and HIS THREE FRIENDS

Punjab

Once upon a time there lived a King and Queen who would have been as happy as the day was long had it not been for this one circumstance,—they had no children.

At last an old *fakír*, or devotee, coming to the palace, asked to see the Queen, and giving her some barleycorns, told her to eat them and cease weeping, for in nine months she would have a beautiful little son. The Queen ate the barleycorns, and sure enough after nine months she bore the most charming, lovely, splendid Prince that ever was seen, who was called Lionheart, because he was so brave and strong.

Now when he grew up to man's estate, Prince Lionheart grew restless also, and was for ever begging his father the King to allow him to travel in the wide world and seek adventures. The King would shake his head, saying *only* sons were too precious to be turned adrift; but at last, seeing the young Prince could think of nothing else, he gave his consent, and Prince Lionheart set off on his travels, taking no one with him but his three companions, the Knifegrinder, the Blacksmith, and the Carpenter.

Now when these four valiant young men had gone a short distance, they came upon a magnificent city, lying deserted and desolate in the wilderness. Passing through it they saw tall houses, broad bazars, shops still full of goods, everything pointing to a large and wealthy population, but neither in street nor house was a human being to be seen. This astonished them very much, until the Knifegrinder, clapping his hand to his forehead, said, "I remember! This must be the city I have heard about, where a demon lives who will let no one dwell in peace. We had best be off!"

"Not a bit of it!" cried Prince Lionheart. "At any rate not until I've had my dinner, for I am just desperately hungry!"

So they went to the shops, and bought all they required, laying the proper price for each thing on the counters just as if the shopkeepers had been there. Then going to the palace, which stood in the middle of the town, Prince Lionheart bade the Knifegrinder prepare the dinner, whilst he and his other companions took a further look at the city.

No sooner had they set off, than the Knifegrinder, going to the kitchen, began to cook the food. It sent up a savoury smell, and the Knifegrinder was just thinking how nice it would taste, when he saw a little figure beside him, clad in armour, with sword and lance, and riding on a gaily-caparisoned mouse.

"Give me my dinner!" cried the mannikin, angrily shaking his lance.

"*Your* dinner! Come, that is a joke!" quoth the Knifegrinder, laughing.

"Give it me at once!" cried the little warrior in a louder voice, "or I'll hang you to the nearest *pipal* tree!"

"Wah! whipper-snapper!" replied the valiant Knifegrander, "come a little nearer, and let me squash you between finger and thumb!"

At these words the mannikin suddenly shot up into a terribly tall demon, whereupon the Knifegrinder's courage disappeared, and, falling on his knees, he begged for mercy. But his piteous cries were of no use, for in a trice he was hung to the topmost branch of the *pipal* tree.

"I'll teach 'em to cook in my kitchen!" growled the demon, as he gobbled up all the cakes and savoury stew. When he had finished every morsel he disappeared.

Now the Knifegrinder wriggled so desperately that the *pipal* branch broke, and he came crashing through the tree to the ground, without much hurt beyond a great fright and a few bruises. However, he was so dreadfully alarmed, that he rushed into the sleeping-room, and rolling himself up in his quilt, shook from head to foot as if he had the ague.

By-and-by in came Prince Lionheart and his companions, all three as hungry as hunters, crying, "Well, jolly Knifegrinder! where's the dinner?"

Whereupon he groaned out from under his quilt, "Don't be angry, for it's nobody's fault; only just as it was ready I got a fit of ague, and as I lay shivering and shaking a dog came in and walked off with everything."

He was afraid that if he told the truth his companions would think him a coward for not fighting the demon.

"What a pity!" cried the Prince, "but we must just cook some more. Here! you Blacksmith! do you prepare the dinner, whilst the Carpenter and I have another look at the city."

Now, no sooner had the Blacksmith begun to sniff the savoury smell, and think how nice the cakes and stew would taste, than the little warrior appeared to him also. And he was quite as brave at first as the Knifegrinder had been, and afterwards he too fell on his knees and prayed for mercy. In fact everything happened to him as it had happened to the Knifegrinder, and when he fell from the tree he too fled into the sleeping-room, and rolling himself in his quilt began to shiver and shake; so that when Prince Lionheart and the Carpenter came back, hungry as hunters, there was no dinner.

Then the Carpenter stayed behind to cook, but he fared no better than the two others, so that when hungry Prince Lionheart returned there were three sick men, shivering and shaking under their quilts, and no dinner. Whereupon the Prince set to work to cook his food himself.

No sooner had it begun to give off a savoury smell than the tiny mouse-warrior appeared, very fierce and valiant.

"Upon my word you are really a very pretty little fellow!" said the Prince in a patronizing way; "and what may you want?"

"Give me my dinner!" shrieked the mannikin.

"It is not *your* dinner, my dear sir, it is *my* dinner!" quoth the Prince; "but to avoid disputes let's fight it out."

Upon this the mouse-warrior began to stretch and grow till he became a terribly tall demon. But instead of falling on his knees begging for mercy, the Prince only burst into a fit of laughter, and said, "My good sir! there is a medium in all things! Just now you were ridiculously small, at present you are absurdly big; but, as you seem to be able to alter your size without much trouble, suppose for once in a way you show some spirit, and become just my size, neither less nor more; then we can settle whose dinner it really is."

The demon could not withstand the Prince's reasoning, so he shrank to an ordinary size, and setting to work with a will, began to tilt at the Prince in fine style. But valiant Lionheart never yielded an inch, and finally, after a terrific battle, slew the demon with his sharp sword.

Then guessing at the truth he roused his three sick friends, saying with a smile, "O ye valiant ones! arise, for I have killed the ague!"

And they got up sheepishly, and fell to praising their leader for his incomparable valour.

After this, Prince Lionheart sent messages to all the inhabitants of the town who had been driven away by the wicked demon, telling them they could return and dwell in safety, on condition of their taking the Knifegrinder as their king, and giving him their richest and most beautiful maiden as a bride.

This they did with great joy, but when the wedding was over, and Prince Lionheart prepared to set out once more on his adventures, the Knifegrinder threw himself before his master, begging to be allowed to accompany him. Prince Lionheart, however, refused the request, bidding him remain to govern his kingdom, and at the same time gave him a barley plant, bidding him tend it very carefully; since so long as it flourished he might be assured his master was alive and well. If, on the contrary, it drooped, then he might know that misfortune was at hand, and set off to help if he chose.

So the Knifegrinder king remained behind with his bride and his barley plant, but Prince Lionheart, the Blacksmith, and the Carpenter set forth on their travels.

By and by they came to another desolate city, lying deserted in the wilderness, and as before they wandered through it, wondering at the tall palaces, the empty streets, and the vacant shops where never a human being was to be seen, until the Blacksmith, suddenly recollecting, said, "I remember now! This must be the city where the awful ghost lives which kills every one. We had best be off!"

"After we have had our dinners!" quoth hungry Lionheart.

So having bought all they required from a vacant shop, putting the proper price of everything on the counter, since there was no shopkeeper, they repaired to the palace, where the Blacksmith was installed as cook, whilst the others looked through the town.

No sooner had the dinner begun to give off an appetising smell than the ghost appeared, in the form of an old woman, awful and forbidding, with black wrinkled skin, and feet turned backwards.

At this sight the valiant Blacksmith never stopped to parley, but fled into another room and bolted the door. Whereupon the ghost ate up the dinner in no time, and disappeared; so when Prince Lionheart and the Carpenter returned, as hungry as hunters, there was no dinner to be found, and no Blacksmith.

Then the Prince bade the Carpenter do the cooking while he went abroad to see the town. But the Carpenter fared no better, for the ghost appeared to him also, so that he fled and locked himself up in another room.

"This is really too bad!" quoth Prince Lionheart, when he returned to find no dinner, no Blacksmith, no Carpenter. Then he began to cook the food himself, and no sooner had it given out a savoury smell than the ghost arrived; this time, however, seeing so handsome a young man before her she would not assume her own hag-like shape, but appeared instead as a beautiful young woman.

However, the Prince was not in the least bit deceived, for he looked down at her feet, and when he saw they were set on hind side before, he knew at once what she was; so drawing his sharp strong sword, he said, "I must trouble you to take your own shape again, as I don't like killing beautiful young women!"

At this the ghost shrieked with rage, and changed into her own loathsome form once more; but at the same moment Prince Lionheart gave one stroke of his sword, and the horrible, awful thing lay dead at his feet.

Then the Blacksmith and the Carpenter crept out of their hiding-places, and the Prince sent messages to all the townsfolk, bidding them come back and dwell in peace, on condition of their making the Blacksmith king, and giving him to wife the prettiest, the richest, and the best-born maiden in the city.

To this they consented with one accord, and after the wedding was over, Prince Lionheart and the Carpenter set forth once more on their travels. The Blacksmith king was loath to let them go without him, but his master gave him also a barley plant, saying, "Water and tend it carefully; for so long as it flourishes you may rest assured I am well and happy; but if it droops, know that I am in trouble, and come to help me."

Prince Lionheart and the Carpenter had not journeyed far ere they came to a big town, where they halted to rest; and as luck would have it the Carpenter fell in love with the fairest maiden in the city, who was as beautiful as the moon and all the stars. He began to sigh and grumble over the good fortune of the Knifegrinder and the Blacksmith, and wish that he too could find a kingdom and a lovely bride, until his master took pity on him, and sending for the chief inhabitants, told them who he was, and ordered them to make the Carpenter king, and marry him to the maiden of his choice.

This order they obeyed, for Prince Lionheart's fame had been noised abroad, and they feared his displeasure; so when the marriage was over, and the Carpenter duly established as king, Prince Lionheart went forth on his journey alone, after giving a barley plant, as he had done before, by which his prosperity or misfortune might be known.

Having journeyed for a long time, he came at last to a river, and as he sat resting on the bank, what was his astonishment to see a ruby of enormous size floating down the stream! Then another, and another drifted past him, each of huge size and glowing hue! Wonderstruck, he determined to find out whence they came. So he travelled up stream for two days and two nights, watching the rubies sweep by in the current, until he came to a beautiful marble palace built close to the water's edge. Gay gardens surrounded it, marble steps led down to the river, where, on a magnificent tree which stretched its branches over the stream, hung a golden basket. Now if Prince Lionheart had been wonderstruck before, what was his astonishment when he saw that the basket contained the head of the most lovely, the most beautiful, the most perfect young Princess that ever was seen! The eyes were closed, the golden hair fluttered in the breeze, and every minute from the slender throat a drop of crimson blood fell into the water, and changing into a ruby, drifted down the stream!

Prince Lionheart was overcome with pity at this heartrending sight; tears rose to his eyes, and he determined to search through the palace for some explanation of the beautiful mysterious head.

So he wandered through richly-decorated marble halls, through carved galleries and spacious corridors, without seeing a living creature, until he came to a sleeping-room hung with silver tissue, and there, on a white satin bed, lay the headless body of a young and beautiful girl! One glance convinced him that it belonged to the exquisite head he had seen swinging in the golden basket by the river side, and, urged by the desire to see the two lovely portions united he set off swiftly to the tree, soon returning with the basket in his hand. He placed the head gently on the severed throat, when, lo and behold! they joined together in a trice and the beautiful maiden started up to life once more. The Prince was overjoyed, and, falling on his knees, begged the lovely girl to tell him who she was, and how she came to be alone in the mysterious palace. She informed him that she was a king's daughter, with whom a wicked Jinn had fallen in love, in consequence of which passion he had carried her off by his magical arts: and being desperately jealous, never left her without first cutting off her head, and hanging it up in the golden basket until his return.

Prince Lionheart, hearing this cruel story, besought the beautiful Princess to fly with him without delay, but she assured him they must first kill the Jinn, or they would never succeed in making their escape. So she promised to coax the Jinn into telling her the secret of his life, and in the meantime bade the Prince cut off her head once more, and replace it in the golden basket, so that her cruel gaoler might not suspect anything.

The poor Prince could hardly bring himself to perform so dreadful a task, but seeing it was absolutely necessary, he shut his eyes from the heart-rending sight, and with one blow of his sharp bright sword cut off his dear Princess's head, and after returning the golden basket to its place, hid himself in a closet hard by the sleeping-room.

By-and-by the Jinn arrived, and, putting on the Princess's head once more, cried angrily, "Fee! fa! fum! This room smells of man's flesh!"

Then the Princess pretended to weep, saying, "Do not be angry with me, good Jinn, for how can I know aught? Am I not dead whilst you are away? Eat me if you like, but do not be angry with me!"

Whereupon the Jinn, who loved her to distraction, swore he would rather die himself than kill her.

"That would be worse for me!" answered the girl, "for if you were to die while you are away from here, it would be very awkward for me: I should be neither dead nor alive."

"Don't distress yourself!" returned the Jinn; "I am not likely to be killed, for my life lies in something very safe."

"I hope so, I am sure!" replied the Princess, "but I believe you only say that to comfort me. I shall never be content until you tell me where it lies, then I can judge for myself if it is safe."

At first the Jinn refused, but the Princess coaxed and wheedled so prettily, and he began to get so very sleepy, that at last he replied, "I shall never be killed except by a Prince called Lionheart; nor by him unless he can find the solitary tree, where a dog and a horse keep sentinel day and night. Even then he must pass these warders unhurt, climb the tree, kill the starling which sits singing in a golden cage on the topmost branch, tear open its crop, and destroy the bumble bee it contains. So I am safe; for it would need a lion's heart, or great wisdom, to reach the tree and overcome its guardians."

"How are they to be overcome?" pleaded the Princess; "tell me that, and I shall be satisfied."

The Jinn, who was more than half asleep, and quite tired of being cross-questioned, answered drowsily, "In front of the horse lies a heap of bones, and in front of the dog a heap of grass. Whoever takes a long stick and changes the heaps, so that the horse has grass, and the dog bones, will have no difficulty in passing."

The Prince, overhearing this, set off at once to find the solitary tree, and ere long discovered it, with a savage horse and furious dog keeping watch and ward over it. They, however, became quite mild and meek when they received their proper food, and the Prince without any difficulty climbed the tree, seized the starling, and began to twist its neck. At this moment the Jinn, awakening from sleep, became aware of what was passing, and flew through the air to do battle for his life. The Prince, however, seeing him approach, hastily cut open the bird's crop, seized the bumble bee, and just as the Jinn was alighting on the tree, tore off the insect's wings. The Jinn instantly fell to the ground with a crash, but, determined to kill his enemy, began to climb. Then the Prince twisted off the bee's legs, and lo! the Jinn became legless also; and when the bee's head was torn off, the Jinn's life went out entirely.

So Prince Lionheart returned in triumph to the Princess, who was overjoyed to hear of her tyrant's death. He would have started at once with her to his father's kingdom, but she begged for a little rest, so they stayed in the palace, examining all the riches it contained.

Now one day the Princess went down to the river to bathe, and wash her beautiful golden hair, and as she combed it, one or two long strands came out in the comb, shining and glittering like burnished gold. She was proud of her beautiful hair, and said to herself, "I will not throw these hairs into the river, to sink in the nasty dirty mud," so she made a green cup out of a *pipal* leaf, coiled the golden hairs inside, and set it afloat on the stream.

It so happened that the river, further down, flowed past a royal city, and the King was sailing in his pleasure-boat, when he espied something sparkling like sunlight on the water, and bidding his boatmen row towards it, found the *pipal* leaf cup and the glittering golden hairs.

He thought he had never before seen anything half so beautiful, and determined not to rest day or night until he had found the owner. Therefore he sent for the wisest women in his kingdom, in order to find out where the owner of the glistening golden hair dwelt.

The first wise woman said, "If she is on Earth I promise to find her."

The second said, "If she is in Heaven I will tear open the sky and bring her to you."

But the third laughed, saying, "Pooh! if you tear open the sky I will put a patch in it, so that none will be able to tell the new piece from the old."

The King, considering the last wise woman had proved herself to be the cleverest, engaged her to seek for the beautiful owner of the glistening golden hair.

Now as the hairs had been found in the river, the wise woman guessed they must have floated down stream from some place higher up, so she set off in a grand royal boat, and the boatmen rowed and rowed until at last they came in sight of the Jinn's magical marble palace.

Then the cunning wise woman went alone to the steps of the palace, and began to weep and to wail. It so happened that Prince Lionheart had that day gone out hunting, so the Princess was all alone, and having a tender heart, she no sooner heard the old woman weeping than she came out to see what was the matter.

"Mother," said she kindly, "why do you weep?"

"My daughter," cried the wise woman, "I weep to think what will become of you if the handsome Prince is slain by any mischance, and you are left here in the wilderness alone." For the witch knew by her arts all about the Prince.

"Very true!" replied the Princess, wringing her hands; "what a dreadful thing it would be! I never thought of it before!"

All day long she wept over the idea, and at night, when the Prince returned, she told him of her fears; but he laughed at them, saying his life lay in safety, and it was very unlikely any mischance should befall him.

Then the Princess was comforted; only she begged him to tell her wherein it lay, so that she might help to preserve it.

"It lies," returned the Prince, "in my sharp sword, which never fails. If harm were to come to it I should die; nevertheless, by fair means naught can prevail against it, so do not fret, sweetheart!"

"It would be wiser to leave it safe at home when you go hunting," pleaded the Princess, and though Prince Lionheart told her again there was no cause to be alarmed, she made up her mind to have her own way, and the very next morning, when the Prince went a-hunting, she hid his strong sharp sword, and put another in the scabbard, so that he was none the wiser.

So when the wise woman came once more and wept on the marble stairs, the Princess called to her joyfully, "Don't cry, mother!—the Prince's life is safe to-day. It lies in his sword, and that is hidden away in my cupboard."

Then the wicked old hag waited until the Princess took her noonday sleep, and when everything was quiet she stole to the cupboard, took the sword, made a fierce fire, and placed the sharp shining blade in the glowing embers. As it grew hotter and hotter, Prince Lionheart felt a burning fever creep over his body, and knowing the magical property of his sword, drew it out to see if aught had befallen it, and lo! it was not his own sword, but a changeling! He cried aloud, "I am undone! I am undone!" and galloped homewards. But the wise woman blew up the fire so quickly that the sword became red-hot ere Prince Lionheart could arrive, and just as he appeared on the other side of the stream, a rivet came out of the sword hilt, which rolled off, and so did the Prince's head.

Then the wise woman, going to the Princess, said, "Daughter! see how tangled your beautiful hair is after your sleep! Let me wash and dress it against your husband's return." So they went down the marble steps to the river; but the wise woman said, "Step into my boat, sweetheart; the water is clearer on the farther side."

And then, whilst the Princess's long golden hair was all over her eyes like a veil, so that she could not see, the wicked old hag loosed the boat, which went drifting down stream.

In vain the Princess wept and wailed; all she could do was to make a great vow, saying, "O you shameless old thing! You are taking me away to some king's palace, I know; but no matter who he may be, I swear not to look on his face for twelve years!"

At last they arrived at the royal city, greatly to the King's delight; but when he found how solemn an oath the Princess had taken, he built her a high tower, where she lived all alone. No one save the hewers of wood and drawers of water were allowed even to enter the courtyard surrounding it, so there she lived and wept over her lost Lionheart.

Now when the Prince's head had rolled off in that shocking manner, the barley plant he had given to the Knifegrinder king suddenly snapped right in two, so that the ear fell to the ground.

This greatly troubled the faithful Knifegrinder, who immediately guessed some terrible disaster had overtaken his dear Prince. He gathered an army without delay, and set off in aid, meeting on the way with the Blacksmith and the Carpenter kings, who were both on the same errand. When it became evident that the three barley plants had fallen at the self-same moment, the three friends feared the worst, and were not surprised when, after long journeying, they found the Prince's body, all burnt and blistered, lying by the river-side, and his head close to it. Knowing the magical properties of the sword, they looked for it at once, and when they found a changeling in its place their hearts sank indeed! They lifted the body, and carried it to the palace, intending to weep and wail over it, when, lo! they found the real sword, all blistered and burnt, in a heap of ashes, the rivet gone, the hilt lying beside it.

"That is soon mended!" cried the Blacksmith king; so he blew up the fire, forged a rivet, and fastened the hilt to the blade. No sooner had he done so than the Prince's head grew to his shoulders as firm as ever.

"My turn now!" quoth the Knifegrinder king; and he spun his wheel so deftly that the blisters and stains disappeared like magic, and the sword was soon as bright as ever. And as he spun his wheel, the burns and scars disappeared likewise from Prince Lionheart's body, until at last the Prince sat up alive, as handsome as before.

"Where is my Princess?" he cried, the very first thing, and then told his friends of all that had passed.

"It is my turn now!" quoth the Carpenter king gleefully; "give me your sword, and I will fetch the Princess back in no time."

So he set off with the bright strong sword in his hand to find the lost Princess. Ere long he came to the royal city, and noticing a tall new-built tower, inquired who dwelt within. When the townspeople told him it was a strange Princess, who was kept in such close imprisonment that no one but hewers of wood and drawers of water were allowed even to enter the court-yard, he was certain it must be she whom he sought. However, to make sure, he disguised himself as a woodman, and going beneath the windows, cried, "Wood! wood! Fifteen gold pieces for this bundle of wood!"

The Princess, who was sitting on the roof, taking the air, bade her servant ask what sort of wood it was to make it so expensive.

"It is only firewood," answered the disguised Carpenter, "but it was cut with this sharp bright sword!"

Hearing these words, the Princess, with a beating heart, peered through the parapet, and recognized Prince Lionheart's sword. So she bade her servant inquire if the woodman had anything else to sell, and he replied that he had a wonderful flying palanquin, which he would show to the Princess if she wished it, when she walked in the garden at evening.

She agreed to the proposal, and the Carpenter spent all the day in fashioning a marvellous palanquin. This he took with him to the tower garden, saying, "Seat yourself in it, my Princess, and try how well it flies."

But the King's sister, who was there, said the Princess must not go alone, so she got in also, and so did the wicked wise woman. Then the Carpenter king jumped up outside, and immediately the palanquin began to fly higher and higher, like a bird.

"I have had enough!—let us go down," said the King's sister after a time.

Whereupon the Carpenter seized her by the waist, and threw her overboard, just as they were sailing above the river, so that she was drowned; but he waited until they were just above the high tower before he threw down the wicked wise woman, so that she got finely smashed on the stones.

Then the palanquin flew straight to the Jinn's magical marble palace, where Prince Lionheart, who had been awaiting the Carpenter king's arrival with the greatest impatience, was overjoyed to see his Princess once more, and set off, escorted by his three companion kings, to his father's dominions. But when the poor old king, who had very much aged since his son's departure, saw the three armies coming, he made sure they were an invading force, so he went out to meet them, and said, "Take all my riches, but leave my poor people in peace, for I am old, and cannot fight. Had my dear brave son Lionheart been with me, it would have been a different affair, but he left us years ago, and no one has heard aught of him since."

On this, the Prince flung himself on his father's neck, and told him all that had occurred, and how these were his three old friends—the Knifegrinder, the Blacksmith, and the Carpenter. This greatly delighted the old man, but when he saw the golden-haired bride his son had brought home, his joy knew no bounds.

So everybody was pleased, and lived happily ever after.

watchmen to climb the roof and open the latch from the inside. Meanwhile the whole village—men, women and children—stood before the beggar's house to see what had taken place inside. The watchmen jumped into the house, and to their horror found the beggar and his wife stretched on opposite verandahs like two corpses. They opened the door, and the whole village rushed in. They, too, saw the beggar and his wife lying so still that they thought them to be dead. And though the beggar pair had heard everything that passed around them, neither would open an eye or speak. For whoever did it first would get only two muffins!

At the public expense of the village two green litters of bamboo and cocoanut leaves were prepared on which to remove the unfortunate pair to the cremation-ground. "How loving they must have been to have died together like this!" said some of the greybeards of the village.

In time the cremation-ground was reached, and the village watchmen had collected a score of dried cowdung-cakes and a bundle of fire-wood from each house for the funeral pyre.[1] From these charitable contributions two pyres had been prepared, one for the man and one for the woman. The pyres were then lighted, and when the fire approached his leg, the man thought it time to give up the ordeal and to be satisfied with only two muffins! So while the villagers were still continuing the funeral rites, they suddenly heard a voice:—

"I shall be satisfied with two muffins!"

Immediately another voice replied from the woman's pyre:—

"I have gained the day; let me have the three!"

The villagers were amazed and ran away. One bold man alone stood face to face with the supposed dead husband and wife. He was a bold man, indeed, for when a dead man or a man supposed to have died comes to life village people consider him to be a ghost. However, this bold villager

---

1.   The village custom in South India when a death occurs in the village.

questioned the beggars until he came to know their story. He then went after the runaways and related to them the whole story of the five muffins to their great amazement.

But what was to be done to the people who had thus voluntarily faced death out of a love for muffins? Persons who had ascended the green litter and slept on the funeral pyre could never come back to the village! If they did the whole village would perish. So the elders built a small hut in a deserted meadow outside the village and made the beggar and his wife live there.

Ever after that memorable day our hero and his wife were called the muffin beggar and the muffin beggar's wife, and many old ladies and young children from the village used to bring them muffins in the morning and evening, out of pity for them—for had they not loved muffins so much that they underwent death in life?

A NOTE ON THE SOURCES

The stories in this book were collected, translated, and published in the late nineteenth and early twentieth centuries. The folklorists included both Indian and British citizens, who drew on interviews with village storytellers and, in the case of Paṇḍit S. M. Naṭêśa Sâstrî, on his own childhood memories as sources for the stories. Although many of these tales appear in multiple variations across India, the particular versions included here were told in the three regions that are now Bengal, Punjab, and Tamil Nadu. These stories were excerpted from the following publications, all of which are in the public domain:

Day, Lal Behari, *Folk-Tales of Bengal*. London: Macmillan and Co., 1883, Internet Archive, 2008. https://archive.org/details/folktalesbengal00daygoog

Naṭêśa Sâstrî, S. M., *Folkore in Southern India*. Bombay: Education Society's Press, 1884-88, Internet Archive, 2009. https://archive.org/details/cu31924024159661

Steel, Flora Annie, *Tales of the Punjab: Told by the People*. Notes by R. C. Temple. London: Macmillan and Co., 1917, Internet Archive, 2007. https://archive.org/details/talesofpunjabtol00stee

Swynnerton, Charles, *Indian Nights' Entertainment; or, Folk-Tales from the Upper Indus*. London: Elliot Stock, 1892, Internet Archive, 2009. https://archive.org/details/cu31924023651072

SOURCES

The Bear's Bad Bargain
From *Tales of the Punjab: Told by the People*, by Flora Annie Steel, with notes by R. C. Temple

The Beggar and the Five Muffins
From *Folklore in Southern India*, by Paṇḍit S. M. Naṭêśa Sâstrî

Bopolûchî
From *Tales of the Punjab: Told by the People*, by Flora Annie Steel, with notes by R. C. Temple

The Brâhmaṇ Girl That Married a Tiger
From *Folklore in Southern India*, by Paṇḍit S. M. Naṭêśa Sâstrî

The Brahmarâkshasa
From *Folklore in Southern India*, by Paṇḍit S. M. Naṭêśa Sâstrî

Eesara and Caneesara
From *Indian Nights' Entertainment; or, Folk-Tales from the Upper Indus*, by Rev. Charles Swynnerton, F.S.A.

Gholâm Badshah and His Son Ghool
From *Indian Nights' Entertainment; or, Folk-Tales from the Upper Indus*, by Rev. Charles Swynnerton, F.S.A.

The Ghost-Brahman
From *Folk-Tales of Bengal*, by Rev. Lal Behari Day

The Indigent Brahman
From *Folk-Tales of Bengal*, by Rev. Lal Behari Day

The King and the Robbers
From *Indian Nights' Entertainment; or, Folk-Tales from the Upper Indus*, by Rev. Charles Swynnerton, F.S.A.

Life's Secret
From *Folk-Tales of Bengal*, by Rev. Lal Behari Day

The Lord of Death
From *Tales of the Punjab: Told by the People*, by Flora Annie Steel, with notes by R. C. Temple

Prince Lionheart and His Three Friends
From *Tales of the Punjab: Told by the People*, by Flora Annie Steel, with notes by R. C. Temple

The Rat's Wedding
From *Tales of the Punjab: Told by the People*, by Flora Annie Steel, with notes by R. C. Temple

The Son of Seven Mothers
From *Tales of the Punjab: Told by the People*, by Flora Annie Steel, with notes by R. C. Temple

The Soothsayer's Son
From *Folklore in Southern India*, by Paṇḍit S. M. Naṭêśa Sâstrî